Kim —

Continued

blessings to you!

Jessica Tilles 7-26-05

Sweet

Revenge

ALSO BY JESSICA TILLES

Anything Goes

In My Sisters' Corner

Apple Tree

JESSICA TILLES

Sweet

Revenge

Xpress Yourself Publishing, LLC

Published by Xpress Yourself Publishing, LLC
P.O. Box 1615, Upper Marlboro, Maryland 20773, U.S.A.
www.xpressyourselfpublishing.org

ISBN: 0-9722990-3-3

Printed in the United States of America
Set in Caslon
Designed by J. Esther Wright

This one's for my road dawg
Jo Hawley Chubbs

Acknowledgements

Unlike my other books, it took me close to a year to complete this one. I absolutely loathed writing this sequel—afraid it would not measure up to the original. Nonetheless, it's completed and I'm indebted to quite a few folks who hung in there with me and kept me sane during the writing of this book.

Thanks to Gary Johnson, Founder and Publisher of Black Men In America.com. You are one of the most sincere and honest people I know. Not only are you a wonderful business partner, it is an honor to call you my friend. I can't thank you enough for opening the door to endless opportunities, being hard on me, and giving me solid criticism. I look forward to a long lasting business relationship, as well as friendship.

Thanks to Carla M. Dean, CEO and Editor of U Can Mark My Word. I am so grateful for you. You work tirelessly to meet my short notice deadlines and your patience is insurmountable. You make me look good!

Thanks to Mom and Dad—Jesse and Wallace Wright—for being a wonderful blessing from God. Your support and motivation is like no other. I love, cherish, and honor you both.

Thanks to Teresa Clark, Glenda Barlow, and Shari L. McCoy for reading the first ten chapters and letting me know I was on the right track. You wanted more, but I didn't want to spoil it for you. There's nothing like reading the finished product.

I am grateful to The McDonald Group, my agent, for having faith in my work and helping me to excel to the next level.

What would I do without Karibu Books? Thank you Simba, Yao, Sunny, Lee, and the entire staff for taking a chance and showcasing my work in all four of your locations. Each and every time I walk through your doors, you always make me feel like a big-time celebrity!

Thanks to all of the book clubs. You read my work and provide me with constructive criticism and wonderful book discussions. A special thank you to the Jackson Mississippi Readers Club in Jackson, Mississippi, aka the Jackson Divas! I love you ladies just as much as you love me.

Thanks to Victor Tilles for remaining in my comfort zone, being the shoulder I can rely on and a true friend. One day, when you least expect it—Porsche!

Thanks to my brother and best friend, Herbert Lipscomb. You have the gift and I am going to help you hone it. *Last Request* will be a bestseller!

Leslie Martin—there isn't anything I can say now that I haven't said during our thirty plus years of friendship. You and I are as close as sisters can be, without the same blood running through our veins. You know me better than anyone, and that sure is a scary thought. Love you!

Thank you John Hampton. You mean more to me than you realize. You set the standard. It is because of you that I have grown into the new woman that I am today. Thanks for the direct line. Whenever I'm feeling blue, I can count on you to cheer me up by saying, "It's going to be okay, Lil' Mama." I'll see you in three years to make good on our pact. *smile*

Lastly, I would like to thank Raven Ward and Morgan Carrington for changing my life in 2002. You consumed my dreams and made me blush with your hot, sizzling tales of *Anything Goes*. Now, my heart is heavy because you're saying goodbye with *Sweet Revenge*. Maybe our paths will cross again someday.

Author's Note

To everyone who sent emails, stopped me in the grocery store, interrupted my dinner dates (trust me, some of those dates needed to be interrupted), and attended my signings, be careful what you ask for. You aren't always going to be able to handle the end result. Remember, hell hath no fury like a woman scorned.

If you are reading this novel, chances are you've already read *Anything Goes*. If not, you're in for a treat. However, in order for you to fully understand what makes Raven tick, you must read *Anything Goes*. Additionally, I am starting this novel with the last chapter of *Anything Goes,* with a few changes, of course. Not too much background history from *Anything Goes*. I'm getting straight to the nitty gritty.

So, sit back, kick up your feet, and grab a glass of something strong (I prefer Crown Royal), and enjoy *Sweet Revenge.*

Sweet Revenge

Chapter 1

Sweat glistened Ramone's bruised naked body. With his wrists and ankles secured to the four-poster bed, Raven drilled into his asshole vigorously and frequently. The strap-on dildo had become an extension of her. The role of dominatrix took her higher than a Philly blunt bursting at the seam with marijuana laced with crack.

A wicked grin crossed her lips as she hung up the phone. "Good boy," she said, patting Ramone on the top of his head like a raggedy ass dog. "Now, while we are waiting for your whorish ass wife, who likes to pick up married men in bars, I'm going to take a shower. The smell of you makes me want to puke," she spewed, her venom more poisonous than a snake.

"Ray, aren't you going to untie me?"

Raven looked over her shoulder and smirked. "Do I look like a fucking fool to you?"

"Please, Ray, I'm in so much pain."

"Good!"

"Please, Ray."

She faced him and leaned against the wall with her arms folded across her chest. "Ramone, I don't give a rat's ass if you're in pain."

For an instant, Ramone became enraged. "You crazy bitch, I was good to you! Why are you doing this?"

She strolled toward the satchel bag sitting next to the nightstand. Reaching inside the satchel, she retrieved the .22-caliber from its holster.

Ramone's eyes widened and flooded with fear and tears.

She squatted down before him. "Ramone, did you really think you could get away with lying to me?"

"Oh God, please don't kill me," he cried. "I was wrong for not telling you about Reneè, but I didn't think it would've made a difference. You said you only wanted the dick and nothing more," he sobbed.

"Ramone, you hurt me. I gave myself to you for three years. You did things to me I would've never allowed anyone to do to me. You brought another man into my home to fuck me while you watched."

"But I thought it was what you wanted?"

"Yes, and thanks to you, I'm with Chas now."

"Fuck Chas."

She waved her index finger in his face, in a 'shame-on-you' fashion. "Ooh, that's not very nice of you, Ramone."

"Man, why did he have to go and tap my pussy?"

"You're the one who led the horse to the water. He simply took a drink."

"He will never be me," he snarled, his body heaving with anger.

"You're right once again. Chas will never be like you because he has what you don't."

"Yeah, and what's that?"

"Me." She smiled as her eyes roamed his body, finally meeting his glare without flinching.

Raven loved sexing Ramone more than eating. He did things to her that made her lose her mind. However, he had to mess it up by not telling her he was married. As far as she was concerned, Ramone was no different than Jay, the no-good bastard who jilted her at the altar.

"Bitch, you are old news. Yeah, I had my way with you. I fucked you when and where I wanted. You're the dumb bitch for allowing me to do it to your ass."

Raven's brow raised in anger. "I *suggest* you *shut* the fuck up," she spoke between clinched teeth. His words had gotten her hotter than hell and her trigger finger had started to itch.

He ignored her word of caution and continued taunting her. "Yeah, I did what the fuck I wanted to do to you," he cackled. "Remember the time you got on your knees and sucked my dick in a pissy ass alley in Anacostia?"

Raven grimaced at the thought. She remembered all too well. It was during a time when she ate, slept, and shitted Ramone. Everything he asked of her, she accommodated.

"Uh huh, and since we're going back down memory lane, remember the time I took you over to my boy's crib and the fellas ran a train on your freak nasty ass?" His laughter was uncontrollable, reminiscent of the Joker from Batman & Robin.

She slowly stood up. Her chest heaved with each deep breath she took. She felt her pressure rising. Sweat began to bead on her forehead. "Yes, I remember," she whispered as she hovered over him. She forced a smile. "Those were the good old days."

"I fucked your ass royally and you loved it. The only difference between you and those tricks on 14th and U Streets is you do it for free, you dumb bitch!" He spat in her face, leaving her with the burning desire to end his life. "Chas can have your used up ass. Your shit's been stretched so wide, it's like the fucking black hole." He laughed hysterically in her face. "You used to be tight. Now my dick gets lost up in ya!" He hollered with laughter to the top of his lungs. He lowered his head and raised his brow. His eyeballs rolled up toward the ceiling, almost rolling to the back of his head, showing only the whites of his eyes. "You better kill me, girl," he snarled. "If you let me loose, I will kill you for sure."

Ramone's words stung deep and the blood running through her veins was at its boiling point. Her hands shook and her knees weakened. She felt like she was on shaky ground. She felt queasy and her breathing turned into short pants. Nevertheless, she maintained her cool.

"Anything else you need to get off your chest, baby?" she asked, reaching for the pillow lying beside Ramone's bruised head.

With uncontrollable laughter, barely getting his words out, he said, "Yeah, does Arthur know you and Morgan be swapping pussy juices? If you can get nasty with that Marcy chick, I know you wouldn't have a problem doing your sister." Ramone went for the jugular and attacked the one person in her life who meant the world to her. He demeaned her sister in one breath. There was no way in hell she was going to let him get away with it. She ignored the Marcy comment. She knew he had probably heard it from Chas.

Raven held the pillow close to her chest and Ramone knew his fate as he pleaded to have his life spared. "Look, man, don't do this. I have two kids, Raven. They can't be without their daddy."

Raven tilted her head back and released a deep sigh. "They were without their daddy every night you spent in my bed."

"Please don't do this!" he hollered as loud as he could, in hopes that someone would hear him. "Oh God, please, Raven!! Oh God, I am so sorry. I was wrong. I promise I won't do anything to you and I will leave you be if you'll let me live, please. I'm begging you, Ray!" Panic like he'd never known welled in his throat, causing him to choke.

Raven was unnerved by Ramone's plead for his life. She placed the pillow over his head, smothering his cries. She wrapped her hands around the gun and lowered it into the pillow, pressing it against the back of his head. She bit down hard on her lower lip and closed her eyes.

BANG!

Ramone's body jolted and then went limp from the muffled gunshot to the back of the head. Blood splattered against the headboard. The white cotton sheets became the canvas for Raven's handiwork, a collage of red spots, streaks, and brain matter.

"Look at what you made me do," she said to the bloodstained pillow. Her voice was emotionless. "I told you to stop running your mouth."

In the blink of an eye, Ramone was face-to-face with his maker.

Raven wanted to call Morgan, but her sister's words played over and over in her head, haunting her. "Ray, it is time for you to stand up and take responsibility for your own actions," Morgan had scolded when she was at her wits end with Raven's behavior. "I don't care how you do it, but you need to do it and do it without me. You don't think about anyone but yourself."

"Stop, stop, stop!" she yelled, her palms plastered to her ears. "Leave me alone!"

Feeling about ready for a straightjacket, Raven took several deep breaths and gathered her composure. She needed to clean the place up. What was she going to do with the body? Her eyes frantically cased the room.

She darted to the bathroom, grabbed a towel, and dampened it with hot, soapy water. She wiped down everything she touched, from the bed, to the nightstand, to the doorknobs. She gathered her belongings and ran around the room frantically, like Ms. Celie trying to get away from Mister in *The Color Purple*.

She came to an abrupt halt. She stood beside the bed and grabbed hold of the sheet. Abracadabra! She pulled the bloodied sheet from beneath Ramone's body and shoved it into her satchel. She focused on the comforter. Where in the hell was she going to put it? It was too big for her satchel.

Her attention turned toward the cubbyhole with hangers. She bolted for the cubbyhole and snatched the plastic laundry bag that hung from the wooden hanger. She neatly folded the comforter, shoved it inside the plastic bag, and pulled tightly on the drawstring. It wasn't a perfect fit, but it would have to do.

She stood in the middle of the room, looked around, and confirmed she had cleaned every surface. However, she still felt she had missed something. Then it dawned on her. She had touched Ramone's clothes. She snatched his clothes from the tattered burnt orange-colored chair, jammed them into her satchel, and forced the zipper to zip. The satchel was filled to capacity.

As she proceeded to the door, a knock stopped her in her tracks.

"Damn, who the fuck is it?" she mouthed. She had forgotten about Reneè.

She contemplated whether she should respond to the knock. She desperately wanted to vacate the room. Being so close to Ramone's dead body was a little too close for comfort.

The knock was persistent.

"Ramone, it's Reneè. Open the door."

Raven slowly tiptoed to the door and looked through the peephole. She swallowed hard and squared her shoulders. The door opened slowly and Reneè stood frozen in the doorway.

"Ramone!" she called out as she put one foot in front of the other and slowly walked through the door, almost as if her feet were pulling several pounds of concrete. She was about to speak as the sight of her husband's dead, badly bruised body stopped her in her tracks. She wrapped her arms tightly around her and cried out like a wounded animal, "Oh my God!" She stood motionless in the middle of the room. Although the pillow was over her husband's head, she knew his lean, muscular body quite well. Thoughts ran rampant through her mind. She didn't know what to do. She was afraid to move. The door slammed and startled her.

Raven stood face-to-face before her enemy. "Hello Reneè."
She walked toward the bed. "Well, you finally made it. You almost
missed me."

Reneè took her stare off Ramone's corpse and directed it
toward Raven. "Did you do this?"

"Naw, he did it to himself." She dropped her hands to her
side. "He was a bad boy and he had to be punished." She shrugged
her shoulders. "Discipline is a bitch."

Reneè stood in shock. Her eyes moved from Raven, to the
door, to the phone. She looked confused.

"If I were you, I would think twice about reaching for the
phone or the door. I'm pretty much shit intolerant, as you can
see." Raven pointed at Ramone's corpse.

Reneè slowly walked over to the bed and knelt down beside
her husband. "But why? I don't understand."

"Sure you do. You understand fully. From what I hear, you
know all about me."

A puzzled look flashed across Reneè's face. "Are you Raven?"

"Who else would it be?"

"I can't believe you did this."

"Listen, the way I see it, you have three choices. One, I can
keep you alive and spend the rest of my life behind bars for killing
your two-timing husband, and that isn't going to happen." Raven
pulled the .22-caliber from the satchel and walked around the bed
to where Reneè stood. "Two, I can have you lie face down beside
him, place a pillow over your head, and you two can spend the
rest of eternity in hell." She picked up a pillow. "Or three, I can

have you lie face up on the bed, place the pillow over your face and shoot you in the head, then place the gun in your hand and call it a murder suicide."

"You have it all planned out, huh?" Reneè stuttered, wringing her hands together. "You will never get away with this."

"Yada, yada, yada…what will it be, one, two, or three?"

"I prefer four," Reneè shouted as she jumped to her feet and kicked her right leg toward Raven's face, attempting to knock the gun from her hand. Unfortunately, she slipped up and knocked her head against the corner of the oak-carved nightstand and fell unconscious.

Raven looked down at Reneè with a questionable look. "Now why would you go and do some dumb shit like that?" Raven grabbed Reneè by her weave and lifted her to the bed, lying her face up beside her beloved Ramone. She wrinkled up her nose at the smell of intercourse around Reneè's mouth. She placed the pillow over her face. "Enjoy hell, bitch," she snarled as she pulled the trigger, firing a muffled gunshot to the side of Reneè's head.

Raven used soap and water to wipe down the gun and placed it in Reneè's hand. *It's a good thing I purchased the gun from off the streets*, she thought. *It can't be traced back to me.* She removed the remaining pillowcases, folded them neatly, and shoved them inside her purse since there was no room in her satchel.

Raven tossed her satchel over her shoulder, and then used the bottom of her shirt to open the door. With her back to the hallway, she took one last glance over the room. When she closed the door and turned around, she came face-to-face with Arthur.

Arthur peeped over her shoulder and saw the massacre. "Raven, what have you done?"

"What business is it of yours?"

He began to shake as the horrible images of the bodies burned in his mind. "Where are Reneè and Ramone?"

"Oh, so now you are concerned about Reneè? I thought you wanted her out of the picture, Arthur?"

"Well, yes, but I didn't want any harm to come to her either."

"Ha! It's too late, babe."

"What do you mean?"

"You shouldn't have fucked her, Arthur!"

"I didn't…"

A muscle quivered in her jaw as she spoke between clinched teeth. "Yes you did! She reeked of cum! You sonofabitch! Did you think to use a fucking condom?"

Arthur stood toe-to-toe with Raven. "Open the door," he demanded.

"Arthur, I suggest you turn yourself around and go home to your wife where you belong. It's your fault I did what I did."

"How is it my fault?"

She grabbed his crotch and squeezed his testicles. "I thought we had an understanding."

"Listen, Raven…"

"No, you listen," she barked. "You will go home to your wife and be the loving husband you've always been, and you will keep your dick in check and never, ever do this shit again. I will go home, shower, relax, and call Chas."

Chapter 2

"I can't believe this," Arthur whined as he slouched in the passenger seat. "I can't believe this."

Air traffic at Reagan National Airport was heavy. The night air, along with the weed wrapping around her lungs, cleared her head.

For the life of me, she thought, *I can't understand why Morgan would be married to such a weak ass man.* Arthur did more whining than an infant. He had gotten on her last nerve. Since she'd begun her romp with Arthur, they'd never talked about anything of substance. When she'd call, he would come, please her, and go home to her sister. It had become boring to her, but she enjoyed the idea of sleeping with her sister's husband, no matter how low and disgusting. She craved him and, although she felt it was getting out of hand, she had no plans of giving him up. Besides, why should her sister have all of the fun? Because of Arthur, she no longer had Ramone and someone had to pick up the slack.

Raven inhaled deeply on the joint. "Well believe it," she exhaled, almost choking.

Arthur began to slowly rock back and forth like a retard.

Raven looked at him, rolled her eyes, and blew smoke in his direction. "Here, take a hit. You need it."

"No!" he snapped. "My life is over." He continued to rock, this time much faster. "I don't do drugs."

"Don't you think you're being a little dramatic?" She was becoming more irritated by the minute with his ass.

"We killed someone," he cried, tears pouring down his face.

"Don't start that crying shit and what do you mean *'we'*?" Raven took one last hit and tossed the roach out the window. She dug inside her purse for a stick of Doublemint gum. "I don't recall *you* doing anything but getting your fuck on." She removed the silver wrapping from the stick of gum and shoved it into her mouth. "Horny ass," she mumbled under her breath.

"I did not…"

"Oh, cut the shit, Arthur."

Arthur fell silent and folded his arms across his chest in a pouting manner.

Raven turned on the radio and tuned it to MAJIC 102.3. The Temptations', *Just My Imagination,* eased her nerves. She was definitely an old school girl. She felt like making a beeline to Tradewinds and doing a little hand dancing. Her co-workers, Jo and Dora, have been trying to get her there for the longest. It was Saturday, she knew they were there, and she was itching to be there, too…anything to get away from Arthur's whining. She didn't know how much more of it she could take before going upside his head.

"What are we going to do?" he sobbed.

The last inch of nerve she had left, Arthur was tap dancing on it. "I don't know about you, but I am going home, take a bath, and call Chas."

"Are you going to tell him?"

"Nope," she said, swaying her head from side to side. "Each day through my window I watch her as she passes by," she sung off key. Her mood had changed for the better. She turned the key from the accessories position to rev up the engine. "Where is your car?"

"I parked in front of the office."

"Why did you park there?"

"I told Reneè I would meet her at the hotel. So, I took the Metro."

"You mind telling me how the plans changed from you taking your ass to the Baltimore Harbor to fucking the bitch at the Renaissance?"

"It was her idea. She suggested we have dinner there. Besides, I didn't know you were going to be there. You said you were going to his house."

Raven glared out the window at the city line of Crystal City shimmering off the Potomac River.

"How did you end up in a room?" She anticipated his response. *This was going to be good*, she thought. He went silent. He resumed rocking back and forth. "Damn it, Arthur, will you stop rocking back and forth like Helen Keller and tell me it was not your idea!" His eyes focused in front of him into the darkness. "What, you got horny for her all of a sudden?"

"I had too much to drink."

"I never thought you would have a problem holding your liquor," she snickered.

"One does if one doesn't drink."

"You got a room and the rest is history."

"So to speak," he whispered.

Raven drove Arthur to his car and dropped him off. But before she pulled off she made one last request. "Arthur, you're going to act as though nothing has happened. Morgan doesn't need to know anything." Arthur stared off into space some damn where. "Do you understand me, man?" she snapped. He didn't budge. She snapped her fingers twice before his eyes. "As long as you keep your mouth shut, we'll be fine. I left no clues…"

"And who the fuck are you, NYPD Blue?" he snapped in return. He jumped out the car and slammed the door. "Oh wait, I forgot about Marcy," he mumbled loud enough for her to hear as he felt around in his pant pockets for his keys.

Raven jumped out of the car and slammed the door. She stormed toward him and stood before him, toe-to-toe and eye-to-eye. "What do you know about Marcy?" she snarled, her good mood now spoiled. "You know, Arthur, I think I've already proven I don't give a fuck. You ought to watch your mouth. Mind whom the fuck you're talking to. I've got too much shit on you as it is."

"Like I don't have shit on you," he shot back, obviously feeling himself. His eyes peered through her. In a matter of minutes, Arthur had grown some balls.

Raven folded her arms across her chest and took a step backward. "Then I don't have to worry about you." She dropped her arms to her side, sashayed to the driver's side, opened the door, and hopped in. Before she rolled up the passenger window, she leaned over and said, "Sweetheart, one more thing."

"What is it?" The tone and posture of his body showed his annoyance with her.

"You need to be at my place tomorrow night at eight o'clock."

Arthur snapped his head toward her and gave her the look of death.

She curled her lips into a smile, blew him a kiss, rolled up the window, and drove off.

Arthur took in deep breaths to calm his nerves. He was whipped and wanted to get home to Morgan. Tonight, he wanted to feel her cuddled up behind him while she snored in his back. He enjoyed the feeling of her round belly nestled behind him. At times, he would feel his offspring pressing against his back.

Arthur couldn't wait to be a father. He'd been preparing himself for the longest. He read every book Dr. Spock had written.

As he smiled at the thought of playing baseball with his son, the cell phone in his jacket pocket blasted to the tune of Nelly's *It's Hot in Herre*. He anxiously grabbed for it, knowing it would be Morgan.

"I think I want to have a baby, too."

Arthur's stomach turned and balled into a big knot. He spoke in a low voice. "Why are you telling me? Shouldn't you inform Chas?"

Raven laughed quietly, almost under her breath. "I want your seed instead."

Arthur shuttered against his will. "You're sick," he said in a slow drawl.

Raven laughed a mechanical laugh and the hair on the back of his neck stood to attention. "Just be ready to give me what I want or else."

"Or else what?" He dreaded her response.

"Or else I'll have to have a talk with Morgan."

Arthur hung up and rushed toward his car. He fumbled with the keys until his shaking hands became steady. He got into the car, dropped his face in the palm of his hands, and cried for an hour before heading home.

Chapter 3

At the Renaissance Hotel on Ninth Street, across from the prestigious Washington Convention Center, a stout Hispanic woman, in her mid-fifties and dressed in a gray maid's uniform, stood before Room 620. The 'Do Not Disturb' sign rested peacefully around the L-shaped door handle.

"Maid service," she announced while knocking.

No response.

She knocked again.

"Maid service!"

With no response, she slid her master key card into the slot. When the green light alerted her the door was unlocked, she turned the handle downward and opened the door. While using her back to hold the door ajar, she retrieved fresh towels and sheets from her cart. She filled her arms with clean linen and backed into the room. She slightly turned her hips and allowed the door to slam shut behind her.

Proceeding left into the bathroom, she rested the fresh towels on the sink. Upon inspection of the bathroom, she noticed the missing towels and washcloths. She shook her head and cursed in her native tongue. It wasn't the first time she'd come across guests who stole towels, washcloths, and anything else that wasn't nailed down from the hotel.

She neatly folded the fresh towels and placed them on the flat metal rack securely nailed to the wall. She hummed an old tune, briefly taking her back to her homeland. She smiled to herself, took the fresh sheets from the sink, and exited the bathroom.

She turned left into the living area. Ear piercing screams filled the room as neatly folded sheets now laid in a mound on the floor. She collapsed to her knees. "Somebody, please!" she cried, loud and continuous. "Help! Help! Call 9-1-1!"

She jumped to her feet, ran toward the door, and flung it open so hard it left an indention in the wall. "Dead people!" she cried. "Dead people!"

Chapter 4

The Metropolitan Police swarmed the room as they scoured for evidence.

Yellow crime scene tape kept away the lookie-loos drawn by the commotion and smell of partially decomposed bodies.

"Lovett, are you coming up with anything?"

"Nothing." Lovett turned toward the corpses. "Mike, what does it look like to you?"

"Looks like someone had a serious vendetta against old boy. Did you see his rectum?" Detective Mike Martin rubbed the back of his neck, hoping to release the built-up tension. "Two bodies, one facedown, the other face-up, and both with pillows over their heads. The bed sheets are gone. No prints whatsoever. Looks like someone knew what they were doing."

"Do you think some funny stuff was going on? I mean someone tore this brother's asshole up. Maybe some gay stuff."

Martin tilted his head, contemplating Lovett's observations. "It's possible."

"In all of my career, I've never seen anything like this," Lovett confessed.

Martin chuckled and patted Lovett on the back. "You've been lucky. I've seen much worse."

"Do we have an ID on the victims?" Lovett inquired.

"Reneè and Ramone Jarvis, two kids, lived over in Deanwood. So you think it was some kinky shit going on, huh?"

"I'll bet my next paycheck on it. We'll see what the coroner has to say."

A uniformed police officer dangled a plastic bag before them. "Detective Martin, I think we've got something here."

"What's this?"

"It's the 'Do Not Disturb' sign that was hanging outside of the door. Looks like we might have a couple of prints."

Martin quickly became annoyed. He sucked his teeth and stood in an authoritative manner. "Were you dropped on your head or something?"

"Excuse me, Sir?"

"What is the first rule of securing a crime scene?" The officer lowered his head. "Answer me damn it!"

"Don't touch anything, unless there is an injured person who must be helped and transported at once."

"Then why in the hell do you have evidence dangling in your bare hand?" The officer walked off and handed the evidence to a member of the Major Crime Scene Unit. "Dumb ass…they are graduating anybody from the damn academy these days." Detective Martin turned toward his partner. "Lovett, have you spoken with the maid yet?"

"Not yet."

"Where is she?"

"Downstairs in the manager's office."

"Get her up here. I want to see what she knows."

Ten minutes later, Detective Lovett returned. "This is Mrs. Ramirez. She discovered the bodies."

"Mrs. Ramirez, can you tell us what you saw?"

Mrs. Ramirez stared at the corpses, mouthed a silent prayer, crossed her heart, and mumbled, "The Father, the Son and the Holy Ghost," while vigorously wringing her hands as tears streamed down her cheeks. "I come into room to clean. I see them there. Dead."

"Where did you clean?" Detective Martin asked.

"I put clean towels in bathroom," she cried. "That's all."

"Do you remember seeing anyone leaving or entering this room at all?" Lovett asked.

She shook her head vigorously. "May I go now?"

Detective Martin nodded his head toward Lovett, who escorted Mrs. Ramirez from the crime scene. Before she exited the room, he handed her his card. "If you think of anything at all, Ma'am, please give us a call."

"Sí."

"Send the gun to forensics for prints. The gun was found in Mrs. Jarvis' hand, but it doesn't mean she pulled the trigger," Martin said, walking past Lovett.

"Okay. Where ya going?"

"Taking my wife to dinner."

"Enjoy." Lovett squatted before the oak wood-carved nightstand. "Hey, check this out before you go." Lovett pointed to the bloodstain on the corner of the nightstand. "Looks like someone hit their head."

Detective Martin reached into his pocket and pulled out a latex glove. He slid the glove over his right hand and walked around to the side of the bed where Ramone laid. He removed the pillow and examined the back of Ramone's head. "Only damage here is the bullet hole." He used his gloved hand to examine Ramone's face and forehead. "Nothing out of the ordinary." Then, Detective Martin found himself hovered over Reneè's body, removing the pillow from her face. Tilting her head to the side, he noticed a tiny bloodstain beneath her head. "Check this out, man." He motioned to Lovett. "If he is tied to the bed, facedown, and it looks like someone had been entering through the exit..." He hesitated. So much talk about homosexuality was making him queasy. "How did she get a knot on the back of her head?"

Lovett rose to his feet. "Well, she definitely hit her head because there are strands of hair on the corner of this nightstand."

"Uh huh, sounds like to me there were three in this room. What do you think?"

"It's possible. Not unless she and her hubby got into a struggle."

"With him tied to the bed?"

"Good point. Let's wait to see what forensics comes up with."

"Yeah, I've got to run before Leslie has one of her tantrums. You know how she can be."

"Yep, I've seen her in action."

They both chuckled heartily.

"Give her my love, man."

"Will do."

Chapter 5

Arthur sat in his favorite chair, watching the Channel 5 News as Shawn Yancey reported how the bodies of husband and wife, Ramone and Reneè Jarvis, were found brutally murdered at the Renaissance Hotel.

"The police say they have no suspects at this time," Yancey reported. "More details to follow as we get them."

Arthur grabbed his head and vigorously rubbed his temples. "Damn, double damn!" he shouted. He cringed as a sharp pain shot from one side of his head to the other.

He'd thought about contacting Detective Martin, but he didn't want to bring suspicion to himself. Martin was always suspicious of anyone who asked questions. You could ask if the sun was setting and Martin would want to know why you're asking. As far as Martin was concerned, everyone was a possible suspect, even his mother.

Arthur stood to his feet and paced the floor. "I'm not going to worry about it," he spoke to himself. "After all, I wasn't the one who pulled the trigger. Hell, I wasn't even in the room when it all went down." He stopped abruptly and a smile crossed his face. "If truth be told, I didn't know what Raven was going to do!" he exclaimed. He propped his hands on his hips and looked up at the ceiling. "I can't be placed at the scene... hot damn!"

He rushed to his office, closed the door, and sat behind his desk. He picked up the phone and quickly dialed. His fingertips frantically tapped on the desk as he impatiently waited for an answer. "Come on! Come on, pick up the damn phone!"

The voice seemed out of sorts.

"Get over here, now!" he summonsed and slammed the phone back in its cradle. He rested his chin in the web of his hand and pondered, "Pay back is a bitch!"

Arthur paced the floor for hours, in deep thought, when the doorbell startled him. He rushed to the door and flung it open. "We must talk," he announced, his face distorted with a constipated look.

Raven followed on his heels, her hands waving in the air. "What in the hell is going on, Arthur?"

Arthur proceeded to the kitchen. He opened the refrigerator and pulled out the pitcher of Lipton Iced Tea. "Sit down," he ordered. "Want some tea?"

"No, I don't want any damn tea," she snapped.

Arthur shot her a piercing look that quieted her down.

She pulled the chair out from the table and sat down. She perched her purse on the table and folded her hands before her, resting them on the table. She inhaled deeply. As she began to speak, Arthur silenced her with the wave of the hand.

"It's my turn to speak."

She relaxed her shoulders in defeat and nodded her head. Arthur had the reign and he wasn't going to loosen up.

"Now, the way I see it…" He pulled a glass from the cupboard and poured his tea. "You are in a bind, sweetie." He took a sip from his glass. "Raven, you committed murder. You killed two people."

Raven tilted her head to the side. "Your point is what?"

Arthur sat his glass on the table. He pressed his palms flat against the table and leaned into her. "No more," he said with emphasis.

Raven stood to her feet. Mimicking Arthur, she placed her palms flat against the table and leaned into him.

He could smell the sweetness of her breath and it was driving him crazy.

Raven licked her lips and said, "No more what, baby?"

Arthur's love began to rise. He took a deep breath, but refused to lower his head in defeat. Although he felt himself becoming weaker and weaker as she stroked her top lip with her moist tongue, he was determined to never darken Raven's bed again.

Raven reached out to him and stroked the side of his face.

He smacked at her hand. "Cut it out!"

Raven snickered, leaned in closer, and puckered her lips.

The sweet smell of Alfred Sung's *Shi* nestled in his nostrils and caused his penis to throb.

Raven smiled, stood erect, and pulled her sweat top over her head as Arthur stared at the full cups of her red lace bra. Raven took his hand and filled it with her breast.

Arthur sighed deeply. His member was pointed upright and ready for lift off.

With his hand plastered to her breast, Raven removed her sweatpants and slipped her fingers inside her red lace panties. She smiled, removed her fingers, and gently placed them in Arthur's mouth.

"You love the way I taste, don't you?" She moved in closer. "You want some more?" She removed her panties, revealing a cleanly shaved slit.

Arthur lost it, nodded his head, grabbed her around the waist, and sat her on the table.

Raven stared into his eyes as she reached between her legs and tilted her head back. Releasing a soft moan, she laid back on the table, propping the heels of her feet on the edge.

Arthur placed the palms of his hands on her knees and pressed her legs open. "Spread your lips," he demanded. "You have a beautiful pussy."

Raven smiled and moaned, "Get under the hood."

Arthur lowered his face into her garden and, with the tip of his tongue, stroked her swollen clitoris with light, feathery strokes. She responded to his touch by releasing a loud moan.

After a few minutes, Arthur used his tongue to mimic a penis, thrusting in and out of her wetness.

"Oh yeah," she cooed, her voice trailing off into a series of long, drawn-out moans.

Arthur pulled his tongue from inside her and kissed her swollen bud, gently sucking on it for a while and sending her over the edge into an explosive orgasm.

"Oh, that shit was good!" she exclaimed, lazily fingering her glistening pussy.

Arthur rose to his feet.

"You're not done, are you?"

"What more do you want?"

"Penetration would be nice," she chuckled.

"You aren't going to be satisfied until you ruin everyone's life around you."

Raven wrapped her legs around Arthur's waist and pulled him closer. "Can we talk about this later?" She pressed her wetness against his abdomen.

Arthur took a step backward. "I don't want you anymore."

Raven sat up on the table. "You don't have a choice," she snarled. "Or have you forgotten about Reneè?"

"No, I have not forgotten. But, it's obvious you have."

"Look, Arthur, you like being with me and I like being with you. What is the big fucking deal? Why can't we enjoy each other? There is no harm being done."

"You are so delusional."

Raven hopped off the table. "I don't hear you complaining when you're fucking my brains out."

Arthur lowered his head. "This shit here," he said, poking her in the chest, "is going to end right here and now or else."

"What? What? What are you going to do, Arthur, with your punk ass?"

Arthur's glare peered through her. His expression became cold and distant. "I'll call the police."

Raven laughed hysterically. "You don't have the balls!"

Arthur turned his head and began grinding his back teeth.

"Who do you think Morgan will side with, you or me? Don't be a goddamn fool. Hell, the way I see it, you have the best of both worlds—a wife and a mistress. Besides, you like fucking me!"

"I don't like it."

"Okay, let's not go down this worn-out road again. But I'll tell you this, dear brother-in-law/boyfriend…" She chuckled. "If you try and fuck me, I will fuck you harder, and believe me, you will not like it. Just ask Ramone. Oh wait, you can't ask Ramone. He's dead." She cackled like a mother hen.

Raven dressed and headed for the door. Before leaving, she looked over her shoulder and yelled, "You've got the best of both worlds, so don't fuck it up!"

Arthur returned to his office and tapped his fingers against the massive desk. His mind was working like crazy. He had to do something, but what was he to do? He wasn't about to take the rap for something he didn't do. And he definitely wasn't going to allow his marriage to be ruined.

Chapter 6

Two metal desks, paired together, sat in the middle of chaos. The Fifth Precinct of Washington, DC's Metropolitan Police Department was the nesting home for men in blue uniforms, with silver badges and guns dangling at their sides, as they hurried the 'innocent until proven guilty' inmates to awaiting jail cells.

Detective Lovett leaned back in his chair, propped his feet up on the desk, and stretched his arms above his head. "What next?" he asked, crossing his hands behind his head. He closed his eyes, in hopes of stealing a short nap. He'd been going nonstop for the past twenty-four hours.

"Don't know," Martin responded with his head buried in paperwork.

"This was definitely a professional."

Martin grunted. "How do you figure?"

"The room was stripped bare. No prints, nothing. Not even DNA on the victims."

Martin pulled his head from beneath the pile of papers and leaned back in his chair. He placed his hands over his potbelly while his fingers intertwined. "Yeah, man, this is definitely someone who knows what she's doing."

"What makes you think the killer is a woman?"

"I have a hunch. I can't imagine any man drilling old boy in the ass."

Lovett returned his feet to the floor and hunched over his desk. "What about the coroner's report? Were there any tissues around the rectum?"

"None, which means a dildo was used, which means it was a woman."

"Now how did you come to that theory?"

Martin leaned forward and looked around, as if about to tell a big secret. "You're a man… right?"

"Last time I checked."

"Would you use a dildo?"

Lovett shook his head. "Don't need to."

"I rest my case."

"So, you think Jarvis had an affair?"

"Yes, I do, and he obviously pissed her off."

Lovett chuckled and said, "Hell hath no fury like a woman scorned."

"You've got that shit right. Now all we have to do is find the scorned woman."

"With no prints? Good luck, my man."

Chapter 7

Dora took a sip from her afternoon Apple Martini at Stan's Restaurant. "You should hang out with us at Tradewinds."

"Girl, I am not interested in hanging with men twice my age," Raven objected.

"Those men who are twice your age know how to treat a woman and will buy you drinks till you pass out," Jo chuckled. "Besides, it's not even like that, Raven. All it takes is one time, and you'll be hooked."

Dora reclined back in her seat and slightly tilted her head toward Raven. "Isn't it sad about Marcy?"

Raven's body stiffened. She sat perfectly still.

Jo shoved a forkful of grilled salmon into her mouth and chewed like it was her last meal. "Yeah, well, from what I understand she was into that kinky stuff... dildos and anal beads."

"I heard she swung both ways," Dora chimed in, her eyes piercing through Raven.

Raven didn't utter a word. In fact, she was hoping they would end the discussion of Marcy. She didn't mean for Marcy to commit suicide. Her intentions were to get revenge on Jay. It was Marcy who took it to the next level, so why should she feel any remorse? After all, she wasn't the one who told the idiot to slit her wrist over a man.

Jo finished her salmon, pushed her plate to the side, and retrieved her carton of Newports from her purse.

"Jo, can you hold off on your hourly smoke?" Dora turned up her nose. "I don't feel like smelling that mess."

"Dora, I will gladly move to another table, but I *will* have my *hourly* smoke."

Dora waved her hand at Jo, the jester, and faced Raven. "You and Marcy were close...right?"

"No, we weren't close."

"Oh? Well, Kathy said y'all went to lunch together and..."

"And what are you trying to imply? I don't do pussy," Raven snapped.

"Ooh, girl, bring it back down. I was simply..."

"Simply insinuating, which is something you always do."

Jo interrupted. "All right now, ladies. Let's bring our voices down and, by all means, please don't spoil my lunch with no damn arguing."

"I'm cool." Raven smiled at Jo. "It's all good...right, Dora?" Raven smiled at Dora, flashing a wink that made Dora uncomfortable.

Dora nodded her head and quickly looked away.

Jo snuffed out her half-smoked cigarette and placed her hand on Raven's forearm. "So you're coming on Thursday?"

"I don't know. . ."

"Oh come on! It will be fun."

"It's not fun if you don't know how to hand dance," Dora snarled.

"Shut up, Dora!" Jo stood to her feet. "It's time to get back to work. Raven, you should come, whether you hand dance or not. Don't listen to Old Grouchy."

Dora rolled her eyes, twisted her neck, and stood to her feet. "Jo Ann, I'm not grouchy!"

"Yes, you are," Raven chuckled. "But you're cool with me, girlfriend."

Dora smiled and propped her hands on her curvaceous hips. "Are you going to come or not?"

"Well…"

"What else do you have to do?" Jo inquired.

"What time?"

"We get there right after work…"

Raven scrunched up her nose. "Who goes to the club while the sun is still shining?"

"We do," Dora smirked. "We get there early to get a good seat."

"After work is too early for me. How about I get there around seven-thirty?"

"We'll save you a seat," Jo said, displaying a victorious smile.

"We need to get back. I ain't trying to work late," Dora huffed.

"Come on, Old Grouchy!"

"You need to cut that shit out, Jo!"

Dora leaned against the wall in the lobby of One Thomas Circle. Jo frantically pressed the call button for the elevator, and Raven was in no hurry to get back to work. Actually, she felt like faking an attack of menstrual cramps as an excuse to leave early, but she had done that more times than she could count on one hand. Her boss wasn't the sharpest knife in the drawer, but he surely wasn't a fool.

"Dang, this elevator is slow as shit today," Jo huffed. "I ain't trying to hear David's mouth, that's for sure."

Dora raised her brow and, looking at Raven with uncertainty, said, "Maybe somebody is holding it up."

Raven's eyes nearly popped out her head. If looks could kill, Dora would be crumpled down on the floor in a pool of red. Dora didn't know whom she was messing with, and Raven knew this better than anyone.

"You know how folks be doing that extracurricular activity in the elevator," Dora said.

"Hush, Dora," Jo snapped.

Raven felt warm and sweat beaded on her nose. "I wouldn't know about fucking in no elevator."

"That ain't what I heard," Dora instigated, smiling as she spoke.

"Damn it, Dora, why don't you stop!"

Dora chuckled. "I'm just messing with Raven. No harm meant."

Raven peered through Dora. "No harm taken, *bitch*."

She felt like smacking the piss out of Dora, but she held back for Jo's sake.

Chapter 8

The digital clock on the nightstand flashed 2:15 a.m. Morgan's back was killing her, along with the massive headache she'd been carrying around for a better part of the day. Morgan's tossing and turning stirred Arthur from his slumber.

"What's wrong, Morgan?"

"I can't get comfortable. I must've moved wrong or something because my back hurts."

Arthur turned over onto his back and rested his forearm on his forehead. "How long have you been having these back pains, Morgan?" he asked, sounding annoyed.

What was his problem? After all, she was the one who should be annoyed. It was her cervix that was about to be stretched wide as the Hoover Dam

"Since one o'clock," she snapped. She wasn't in the mood for any of his mess.

Arthur rose up in the bed and clapped his hands twice, turning on the ceiling light. Ever since he had The Clapper installed, it'd been like a toy to him. He loved to recite the commercial. *"Clap on, clap off, The Clapper."* His singing of the jingle always drove Morgan clear up the wall.

"Why didn't you wake me up before now?" he asked in a condescending manner. "You're in labor, Morgan."

"I am? Well shoot, this isn't too bad."

"Right now, it isn't. We'll see how you feel in a few hours." Arthur retrieved his watch from the nightstand. "Okay, I am going to use the stopwatch feature. Let me know when you start getting pains in five minute intervals." Arthur returned the watch to the nightstand, punched his pillow, balled it under his head, exhaled, and resumed his snoring. Sometimes, Morgan felt like stapling his mouth shut. As soon as he would fall asleep, his mouth would drop open and in came the hogs.

Three hours later. Ten minutes apart. The pain really wasn't bad. She was handling it well. The idea of the baby finally coming excited her. She hoped she could be a good mother. She had plenty of experience raising Raven after their parents' death.

Thinking about Raven drifted her thoughts to Marcy. She didn't deserve to die. Yes, she committed suicide, but if Raven weren't so set on getting back at Jay, Marcy would still be alive. So, in a sense, it was Raven's fault she's dead. Marcy's death didn't affect Raven in the least. Oh, she put on a good act with Chas and Arthur, but Morgan knew her little sister all too well. She felt no remorse whatsoever.

Another two hours later, Morgan's contractions were now four minutes apart and hurting like hell. She was afraid and needed someone to talk to.

Not wanting to deal with Arthur, she leaned over, inhaling his night breath, and quickly snatched the cordless phone from its cradle to dial Raven's number.

"It's me. You sleep?"

"I was. Is everything okay?"

"I'm having contractions."

"Are you at the hospital?"

"No, I'm at home. Don't want to go to the hospital just yet, but soon though."

"Where's Arthur?"

"Asleep."

"Well, wake his ass up! He should be…"

"Nope, let him sleep. He'll only get on my nerves. I called you because I wanted to talk."

"Okay. What do you want to talk about?"

"The baby…"

"What about the baby?"

"Can you believe I am about to be a mother?"

"Yes, and I'm glad, too. Maybe you will stop trying to be my mother."

"Someone should be your mother," Morgan chuckled. "You know, Ray, you were a handful. You gave Mama and Daddy a fit, girl."

"I don't know what you're talking about."

"Uh huh, you know what I'm talking about. You were bad as shit and still are," Morgan chuckled between contractions. "Oooh, Lord."

"Everything all right?"

"Yes…a contraction."

"Are you keeping time on them?"

"Yes, I am. Now back to the subject at hand, your bad ass."

"I was no worse than you, Miss Thang," Raven retorted.

"Not as bad as you were. Do you remember what you did to Roscoe?"

"I couldn't stand that damn cat," Raven snapped. "Besides, I didn't throw him in front of the bus. His dumb ass ran across the street. Wasn't my fault he didn't see the bus coming."

Morgan gasped. "Bitch, you chased the cat into the street!"

Raven fell out with laughter. "I did not!"

"You did too! Ooh!" Morgan stifled her laughter and bit down as hard as she could on the pillow. "Whew, that was a big one."

"They hurt that bad, huh?"

"Girl, as much as I wanted to have a baby, I'll never do this again," she laughed. Arthur grunted and turned over. She shot him a smirk and said, "I hope he looks like Arthur."

"Yeah, Arthur is a handsome brother."

"Um hum, I picked a good one, Ray."

Ray sighed with envy. "Yes, you certainly did."

"But anyway, as far as my being your mother, you do need guidance. Enough said."

"Kiss my ass, Morgan," Raven chuckled. "So, what's it like?"

"What, the contractions?"

"Yeah…"

"Well, at first it started out being back pains, and I thought, 'wow, this isn't so bad.' But now, it feels like someone is kicking me in my stomach as hard as they can every so many minutes."

"Are you doing your breathing?"

"Girl, no, I haven't thought about anybody's breathing. When the pain hits, I just grab hold of the pillow and bite down on it and…oh shit, I just peed on myself."

"You what?"

"I just peed on myself. Feels like someone opened up the flood gates between my legs."

"Sounds like your water broke! Wake up Arthur and get your ass to the hospital. I'm on my way."

"On your way where?"

"To the hospital, you fool."

Raven slammed the phone down before Morgan could respond to her 'fool' comment.

Morgan briskly shook Arthur by the shoulder. "Arthur, wake up." He was dead to the world. She smacked him upside his head. "My water broke. It's time."

"You didn't have to hit me!"

"I have no time to argue with you, Arthur. I have to get to the hospital. My water broke, damn it!"

"Okay, don't panic. How do you know it's your water and you just didn't pee on yourself?" His voice was heavy with sarcasm.

Morgan glared at Arthur as if he had lost his mind. "Are you sure you're a doctor?" She snatched the soaked covers off of her. "Don't you see all this white stuff? Does this look like piss to you? Why would you ask me such a dumb ass question, Arthur?"

"Okay. I know you're afraid..."

"Hell yeah, I'm afraid. Get my suitcase from the closet. It's already packed." Understanding her fear, Arthur ignored her tantrum and darted to the closet. "Come help me out of the bed, damn!"

"Look, Morgan..."

"Not now, Arthur. I'm about to have a baby!" She pulled herself out of bed and walked toward Arthur's side of the bed.

"What are you doing?"

"I'm going to call the doctor."

"Why?"

"Because I'm suppose to, or have you forgotten that rule of thumb, too!"

Arthur released a deep sigh of disgust, grabbed the suitcase, and stormed down the stairs.

"Where are you going?" she yelled.

"To warm up the fucking car," he yelled back.

"You don't have to curse at me. All the pain I'm in, I should be the one doing the cursing," Morgan shot back.

Chapter 9

"My sister is about to have a baby!" Raven yelled into Chas' ear while her car sped up North Capitol Street. "Chas wake up, damn it! Morgan is about to give birth!"

"Already? Are you going to the hospital?"

"Yes! That's why I'm calling you!"

"Okay," Chas chuckled. "Calm down, baby. I know you're excited. . ."

"Why wouldn't I be excited? I am going to be an auntie!"

"Well, Auntie Raven, do you want me to meet you at the hospital?"

"You would come?"

"Of course, I would. You think I wouldn't?"

"No, of course. . ."

"You're my woman, Raven. I will always be by your side."

A lump the size of a golf ball formed in her throat, blocking her passage. She couldn't catch her breath. She felt like she was choking.

"Baby, what's wrong? Are you there?"

Raven let out a long, audible breath. "Uh huh, I'm here," was all she could utter.

"Which hospital?"

"Washington Hospital Center, but you don't have to come if you don't want to."

"Woman, please. I'm going to hop in the shower and I will be there as soon as I can. Keep your cell on. I'll call you when I'm on my way."

"Baby, I am so glad you're in my life."

His smile spoke volumes in her ear. "I'm glad you're in my life, too, baby. I'll see you later." Chas kissed the phone and ended the call.

Raven reduced her speed and flipped on MAJIC 102.3 FM, mellowing her nerves with Mike Chase's soothing, make-your-panties-fall-down-around-your-knees, baritone voice.

Chapter 10

Arthur sat angrily in the car and watched Morgan wobble from the house to the car as the contractions kicked her behind.

"Why are you sitting there? Help me!" Arthur grunted and reluctantly got out of the car. "What the hell is wrong with you, Arthur?"

Arthur rushed to the passenger side of the car and opened the door. "I know you're in pain, Morgan, but I will not stand for you being verbally abusive to me."

Morgan stopped in her tracks and stared at Arthur, her eyes squinted and her brow formed into an arch.

"Get in the car, Morgan."

"Motherfucker…"

Arthur raised his hands in the air. "Cut it out, damn it!" He snatched Morgan's purse and tossed it inside the car. "Get your ass in the fucking car!"

"Who do you think you're…?" Morgan lost her balance and fell onto the car. "Oh God!"

"Baby, what's wrong?"

"It hurts so badly, Arthur," she cried, hunching over the hood of the car and holding her stomach.

Arthur reached for her and helped her inside the car. After closing the door, he ran around to the driver's side. He patted his pants pockets and then he felt around in his jacket pockets.

"What are you doing?" Morgan shouted from inside the car.

"I can't find my keys."

"You dumb ass, the fucking car is running!"

Angrily, Arthur got in the car and slammed the door. He put the car in reverse and tore out of the driveway.

"Hey, Mario Andretti, do you mind?" Morgan growled.

Arthur slammed on the brake and slammed his fist against the steering wheel. "Will you *please* shut up?" he snapped. "Damn, Morgan!"

Morgan continued holding her stomach as she peered at Arthur. There she was about to have a baby and he was having temper tantrums. He had much nerve indeed.

"Excuse me?" she asked, her tone chilled.

Arthur took a deep sigh and grabbed tightly to the steering wheel. "I'm sorry. I'm stressing, that's all." He leaned his head back against the headrest. "Put on your seat belt."

Morgan faced forward and didn't budge. "Fine," he muttered as he shifted the car into drive and peeled off down the street toward I-495.

Morgan was fit to be tied. She was so pissed with Arthur, she was able to bear down when a contraction hit and not utter a sound.

As they sat at the traffic light at Pennsylvania Avenue and Suitland Parkway, Arthur asked, "How are you feeling?"

Morgan responded by turning on the radio, the volume higher than normal.

Arthur shook his head in disgust.

When the light turned green, Arthur floored the accelerator, turned left onto Suitland Parkway, and exceeded the fifty miles per hour speed limit.

"Slow down, Arthur! This is not the Indy 500!" Morgan scolded. "Arthur, slow the fuck down!"

The more Morgan mouthed off, the faster Arthur drove. Fear swept through her. Arthur sped the span of Suitland Parkway in five minutes flat, ignoring traffic lights at Naylor and Stanton Roads and the 'speed checked by radar' signs. Morgan's eyes enlarged as their black Mercedes 500 SL approached Firth Sterling Avenue. The traffic light was bright red.

"The light, Arthur!" Morgan braced herself. "People are in the street!" she yelled, followed by a loud scream.

Arthur slammed on the brakes, hoping to stop the car. Instead, the car did a tailspin, first to the left and then to the right. The right fender impacted with the curb, throwing Morgan through the windshield, where she landed on the hood. It was as if everything started happening in slow motion as Arthur watched in horror, but was unable to help. His head banged against the steering wheel and snapped backward. Arthur slowly began to lose consciousness as he thought about his pregnant wife.

"Morgan," he whispered as his eyes closed.

Chapter 11

Raven arrived at Washington Hospital Center, frantic. Morgan and Arthur had not yet arrived.

"What do you mean she's not here? She should be here by now!"

The nurse kept her cool. She was used to dealing with out-of-control family members. "I'm sorry, Ma'am, Mrs. Carrington has not arrived."

Raven propped her hand on her hip and stuck out her neck. "Now you listen to me…"

The nurse wasn't having it. "Ma'am, if you would like to wait in the waiting room, you're welcome to do so. I'm sure she'll be here momentarily."

The nurse turned on her heels and strolled down the hall.

Raven was steaming. She wanted to take off her shoe and throw it at the back of her head, but she knew better. She had to mind her manners.

Raven straightened her posture, adjusted her purse straps over her shoulder, and sashayed, diva style, to the waiting room.

The waiting room was empty and gloomy, with gray carpeting, gray and maroon striped walls and stain-covered gray chairs. *Oh, this is depressing as hell,* she thought.

As she was about to take a seat, she heard the revolving doors open. She darted in the hall and saw Chas.

"Raven," Chas called out, approaching her. "How are you, baby?"

Hysterically, Raven ran toward Chas. "They aren't here yet!"

"They don't live around the corner, baby. It will take them a minute to get here."

Raven rubbed her hands together. Her nerves had gotten the best of her. "I know, but they should've been here by now." She was shaking uncontrollably.

Chas embraced her and whispered in her ear. "Baby, you need to calm down." Resting his arm around her shoulders, he led her back into the waiting room. He spotted the Mr. Coffee on the table across the room. "Would you like a hot cup of coffee?"

Raven shook her head no and took the seat closest to the door. She wanted to be in a position where she could hear Morgan when she arrived.

Raven rocked back and forth. "I know she is so afraid," she said as tears trickled down her cheek, dropping onto her shaking hands.

Chas stood and watched his woman rock back and forth like a disoriented child. Her mental state reminded him of Marcy when she committed suicide. It had pushed Raven over the edge. He and Arthur found her sulking in her apartment, in desperate need of a bath, and with half eaten boxes of pizza strewn about.

Tears streamed down her face as she raised her head and looked at Chas. "Something's wrong. I can feel it."

Chas took the seat beside her and cradled her in his arms. "Hush now. Everything is fine."

"Then why aren't they here?"

"Raven, you're closer to the hospital. They live out near Waldorf, so you know it's going to take them longer. Besides," he chuckled, "Morgan probably has Arthur driving as slow as a snail."

"Yes, I suppose you could be right."

"Of course, I am." He patted the side of her head and gently pushed her head onto his shoulder. "Close your eyes and get some rest, babe."

Chas cuddled Raven and took a deep sigh. He looked down at her, smiled, and kissed her on the forehead.

Chas' kiss felt good to her. She raised her head and grazed his lips with hers.

Chas returned with a peck on her lips, then covering her mouth with his.

Raven wrapped her arms around Chas' neck, pulling up into him. "I'm so glad you're here."

Chas placed his hand on her inner thigh. He gently stroked her thigh, his hand slightly moving up toward her crotch.

Raven slightly opened her legs, letting him find her warmth. Her hands roamed his body, moving downward until she had a hand between his legs. She fumbled with his belt, undoing his pants. There was urgency to what she was doing. She wanted him — now!

He tried to push her hands away from his waist. "Baby, we can't do this here."

She ignored him, her pants low and rough. She lowered herself before him, unzipped his pants, and allowed the tip of his penis to breathe.

Chas looked around the room and toward the door. "Baby, what are you doing? Woman, we can't do this in here."

Again, she ignored him and lowered her head into his abdomen.

Chas' legs stretched out before him, encircling her. His eyes darted toward the entrance of the waiting room. He prayed no one would enter.

"We are going to jail," he said, grabbing the back of her head. He pushed himself deeper into the warmth of her moist mouth, his helmet connecting with her tonsils.

His eyes closed as he stretched his arms above his head, grabbing for something to hold on to. He scraped at the wall instead. "Damn, baby!"

Still affixed to his dick, Raven pulled her pants down around her ankles. She inserted her finger inside her wetness while her thumb played with her clitoris, which had now become a swollen, throbbing knot.

She released him from her grasp and stood to her feet.

Chas slid down in the chair, his behind dangling off the edge.

Raven straddled him and slowly lowered herself onto his hardened shaft. He helped her by using his hand to guide himself inside her. Within seconds, she was moving up and down on him, her head arched back in pleasure. She raised her blouse. Her exposed breast jutted out before her. She lowered herself and her hardened nipples rubbed teasingly against his lips.

He thrust up to meet her and each time she expelled a satisfied moan.

Her breath was short and her body trembled from anticipation of something wonderful.

She let herself down more forcefully onto him and suddenly she stopped and let out a shrill cry of ecstasy.

Chas placed his hand over her mouth. "Not so loud, baby."

The possibility of them being caught in the act excited her. She raised her right arm in the air and wound it up several times. She was the cowgirl and he was her buck. She was going to ride him for all it was worth. Her strokes were more forceful. Her body began to shake uncontrollably.

Chas smiled. He knew Raven all too well. He knew every inch of her body. He knew the exact location of her G-spot and how to hit it properly. He reached down between them and fingered her clit.

As much as she tried to suppress her orgasm, she couldn't hold back. "Yes, motherfucker, yes!"

"Baby, not so loud."

"Don't stop! Don't stop!"

Chas' finger increased in speed.

"That's it. I'm about to cum, baby!" Raven made a scowling noise, close to a wounded animal.

Chas felt her juices squirt against his abdomen and joined her in a long, satisfying climax, leaving them both out of breath and damp with perspiration.

Raven panted like a worn-out dog as she rose to her feet and plopped down in the seat next to Chas. "You know what?"

Chas turned his head toward her. "What?"

"It smells like pussy in here."

The warmth of his smile echoed in his voice. "Lady, you are too much."

Chapter 12

Flashing reds and yellows lit the night sky as Morgan's lifeless body laid sprawled across the hood of the car. The Emergency Response Team worked on her profusely.

"I'm not getting anything," one of them yelled into the night air. "No pulse."

The ERT hurried Morgan into the ambulance and rushed her to the closest hospital, DC General Hospital. They continued to work on her, trying to bring her back to life.

"Come on, Mrs. Carrington, work with me. We can't lose you!"

Two figures stood at the end of a tunnel of light.

Morgan looked with her eyes partly closed. She couldn't make out the figures before her. She walked closer. The closer she walked, the more she could smell the familiar scent of Chanel No. 5. She inhaled deeply and gasped. "Mama? Daddy?"

Her mother took a step closer, leaving the light, and smiled widely. "Hi, Baby! What are you doing here?"

Morgan looked around in a daze. "I don't know. Where am I?"

"Somewhere you shouldn't be," her father responded angrily. "You have to go back now."

Morgan looked behind her and saw darkness. There seemed to be nothing for her to go back to. "But Daddy, I don't want to go back. I want to stay here with you and Mama. I've missed you so much." Her eyes filled with salty tears. She blinked several times for a clearer vision.

Her mother wrapped her arms around her shoulders and embraced her. "It's not your time, sweetheart. Besides, someone has to watch after Raven."

"Raven can take care of herself," Morgan pleaded. "Please, let me stay."

Her father smiled and looked toward her round belly. "Who is going to take care of my grandchild?"

Morgan looked down and touched her belly. She couldn't see her feet. She smiled. She'd almost forgotten about the baby. "Arthur and I decided to name the baby after you, Daddy."

Her father chuckled. "What if the baby ends up being a girl?"

"Then she'll be named after Mama."

Her mother's face softened. She placed one hand over her heart. "What about Arthur, honey? He needs you."

Her father grunted. "Yeah, more now than he ever needed you before."

"What does that mean, Daddy?"

"Nothing, sweetheart," her mother quickly cut in, shooting her husband a nasty look. "You have to go back now."

"But Mama..."

"No, Morgan. We aren't going anywhere. We will see you when it's your time." Her mother kissed her on the forehead, turned her around, and gave her a slight nudge. "Go on now, Morgan."

"Yes, we'll see you when it's your time, baby. And keep an eye on that sister of yours. She's a rotten seed," her father proclaimed.

Morgan snapped around at her father's comment. *Rotten seed,* she thought.

Her mother waved her hand toward her. "Oh, don't pay your father any mind."

Morgan smiled and said, "You both look so good."

"We love you, honey!"

"I love you, too!"

Morgan turned away from the light and walked into the darkness.

Chapter 13

Lying on the gurney, Arthur raised his head in search of Morgan. "Where's my wife?"

He didn't see her anywhere. He couldn't even make out the hospital. His vision was slightly blurred, making it hard for him to differentiate the nurses from the doctors.

The medical staff hurried by him, unintentionally ignoring his question. They all were on a mission. They needed to see to the patients who weren't as lucky as Arthur.

"Morgan Carrington…where is Morgan Carrington?" He continued to ask the location of his wife, but he was still ignored.

By now, Arthur was frustrated and pulled himself up onto his elbows. He looked around at the chaos around him.

"Do you know who I am? I am Dr. Arthur Carrington, goddamn it!"

He forced himself up to a sitting position. He felt woozy and quickly grabbed for his forehead, feeling the bandage wrapped around his head. He slowly lowered his hand and stared at the splotches of blood decorating his palm.

He attempted to stand to his feet, but lost his balance and grabbed on to the gurney. Once he gathered his bearings, he stood upright, squared his shoulders, and walked into drama, trauma, and pure turmoil.

He approached the nurses' station and stood and waited until he was noticed. The nurse never looked up. He knew she knew he was standing there. He hated when nurses did those kinds of things. It was annoying and unprofessional. He decided to speak up.

He cleared his throat and pinched his lips together. "Morgan Carrington, where is she?"

She looked up from her crossword puzzle. "And you are?"

He slightly leaned back and glared at her. "Pardon me?"

"Who are you?" She spoke slowly, as if speaking to a deaf mute.

Arthur couldn't believe his ears. This definitely was not the Washington Hospital Center because the administration did not tolerate such behavior.

She tilted her head to the side. Her face was full of disgust and annoyance. "Uh, hello?"

"You are rude." Arthur enunciated every word with direct authority.

"Excuse me?"

"You're not excused. Who is the supervising physician on duty?"

She sat up straight and glared at Arthur with questionable eyes. "What is it I can help you with?"

Arthur relaxed his posture and leaned on the counter, looking down at her crossword puzzle and then up at her. The angry wrinkles around his eyes had softened. "Are you good at those?"

She smiled and shrugged her shoulders. "I do pretty well."

A psychotic grin formed on his face. "It's a good thing you're good at something because you are one lazy bitch!"

Her mouth dropped to the floor. She wanted to chew into his ass, but she knew she couldn't do it without the possibility of losing her job.

Arthur's demeanor changed drastically. He'd become aggressive and a real smart ass. "Close your mouth. You need to see a dentist."

The nurse gasped and pursed her lips tightly together. Imaginary smoke exuded from her ears and her nose flared like a bull ready to attack.

"I am Dr. Arthur Carrington, head of Oncology at Washington Hospital Center. When I ask you a fucking question, I expect a direct answer. You are rude, disrespectful, and slacking on the job, with your fucking crossword puzzles. So now, I will ask you one more time and you *will* answer the question. Do you understand me?"

She nodded her head, her eyes as wide as ping-pong balls.

"Good. I'm looking for my wife, Morgan Carrington. She's pregnant. We were in a car accident. Where is she?"

She looked to her right and reached for a clipboard. She skimmed over the clipboard and spoke quietly. "She's about to go into delivery."

"Where? Take me there!"

She didn't move.

"Now!"

She jumped from her seat and rushed Arthur to the delivery room.

Arthur's cell phone vibrated on his hip. He spoke into the mouthpiece in a monotone voice. "Yes."

"Arthur!"

"You don't have to yell in my ear, Raven."

"Where are you? I'm at the hospital…"

"DC General, I think."

"What are you doing there? Chas and I are here waiting for you and Morgan. Where is Morgan?" Arthur took a deep sigh and continued following on the heels of the disgruntled nurse. "Arthur, are you still there?"

"We were in an accident…"

"Oh, my God! Oh no, please no!"

"Morgan is fine, as far as I know. I'm on my way to her now. She's in delivery."

"She can't have the baby at DC General!"

"Raven, Morgan was thrown through the windshield. I'm going into delivery now." Raven let out a loud scream. "Oh, cut the drama. I've gotta go." Arthur flipped the phone closed and entered the delivery room.

"Morgan." He walked toward her. "Morgan, baby, can you hear me?"

A young physician approached Arthur. "Are you Dr. Carrington?"

"Yes, I am. What is her condition?"

The doctor shook his head, sighed deeply, and reached for Arthur's hand. "I'm Dr. Struthers. Mrs. Carrington has sustained injuries to the right side of her cerebrum. Although all of her vitals are stable, she may have bleeding due to impact."

Arthur's legs felt weak. His knees buckled. He blamed himself for Morgan's condition. *I did this*, he thought. Arthur dropped to his knees and wept with his face in his hands.

"Oh, my God, what have I done?"

"Dr. Carrington, try and pull it together. We are doing everything we can. We're still in the process of running CT scans and MRIs to confirm the extent of her injuries."

Arthur ceased his cry and looked into Dr. Struthers' eyes. He was looking for a sign. Any sign telling him the child Morgan had planned and lived for was going to be all right.

Arthur tried to regain his composure. He took a big gulp. "The baby?"

"Quite frankly, Dr. Carrington, I've never seen anything like it."

Arthur rose to his feet. "What do you mean?"

"With the trauma your wife sustained, it would appear the baby wouldn't have survived."

"Dr. Struthers, what are you saying?"

"We are ready to take the baby and we need your consent to perform the cesarean."

"What about Morgan?"

"She sustained much trauma to her head. She lost so much blood, which is why we need to take the baby." Dr. Struthers glanced at Morgan as she lay unconscious with tubes coming from her nose and mouth. "However, only time will tell." Sometimes, it was hard for him to control his emotions when dealing with his patients. After all, he was human.

Arthur slowly turned toward Morgan, reached for her hand, and held it in his. "Baby, can you hear me?" He knelt down at her bedside and pleaded for her to open her eyes, to show some sign, anything, letting him know she would be all right. He raised her hand to his lips and softly kissed each finger.

"Dr. Carrington, we need to get started. It won't take long."

Tears flooded his eyes. "I want to stay with her."

Dr. Struthers summonsed the assisting nurse to get Arthur scrubbed and ready.

Chapter 14

Arthur grinned from ear to ear when Franklin Ward Carrington entered the world, weighing in at a hefty eight pounds seven ounces.

Baby Franklin flipped and flapped like a fish out of water as Dr. Struthers held him upside down and smacked him on the behind.

"You hear the lungs on him? A beautiful, healthy baby boy," Dr. Struthers announced.

Arthur smiled when his son tested his vocal cords. "Yes, he's beautiful." He turned to Morgan. "Look, honey, it's our son. He looks just like you, baby."

Arthur's excitement turned to tears from Morgan's unresponsiveness. Fear and guilt danced in his heart. He blamed himself for Morgan's condition. His posture changed as his shoulders slumped and his back curled.

Arthur quickly slid from the operating room and into the hall where he bumped into Raven, causing her to bounce off the wall.

Raven straightened herself and turned up her lips.

Arthur's features hardened. "Don't say one fucking word."

His tone infuriated her. "Excuse me!"

"Not now, Ray." Chas pulled her into him. He caressed her shoulders as he asked Arthur, "How is Morgan?"

Arthur leaned against the wall and propped his hands on his hips. He pressed the bottom of his left shoe against the wall as his body slumped over. Unspoken pain was alive and glowing in his eyes.

Raven's lids slipped down over her eyes. "Oh, my God, Arthur, is she…?"

Arthur raised his hand and quieted her. "No, she's not dead."

She leaned back and propped her head against Chas' shoulder. She took a deep sigh. "Thank you, God."

"She's not out of the woods, though."

Chas faced Arthur and placed his hand on his shoulder. "Art, what do you mean?"

Panic like she never felt before welled in her throat. "Is Morgan going to be all right?"

"I don't know."

Raven slowly moved toward Arthur. "What do you mean you don't know?" She pursed her lips tightly, her mind a mixture of hope and fear. "You're a fucking doctor, aren't you?" She turned her back on him without waiting for a reply. "You sonofabitch, if my sister dies, it will be your fault!"

"Come on, baby. Give the man a break. That's his wife in there."

"And she's my sister!" Raven glared through Arthur and mumbled, "Yeah, I'll give him a break all right. I'll break my foot off in his punk ass."

Arthur's head snapped to attention. "Oh, so now you give a shit about your sister?"

Raven's eyes narrowed. Her lips tightened. "I love my sister."

"You don't love your sister. You don't give a fuck about anyone but your damn self!" Arthur turned and walked away before coming to an abrupt halt. "Not that you give a shit, but you have a healthy nephew." He jammed his hands inside his pants pockets and strolled down the hall.

Chas' posture tightened. "Wait a minute, Arthur! You don't have to speak to my woman in that manner!"

Arthur stopped suddenly and quickly turned on his heels. "Your woman?" He slowly walked toward Chas. "Your woman?" He stood toe-to-toe with Chas and inhaled deeply. His face became distorted. "When you find out about *your woman*, then we can talk."

Chas took a step closer. "What in the hell is that suppose to mean?"

Arthur turned his glare toward Raven. A wicked grin crept across his hardened face.

Raven pressed the palm of her hand against Chas' chest. "Baby, it's okay. Arthur is under stress. He doesn't mean it."

Chas backed down and Arthur wickedly smiled at him.

"Come on, baby. I want to see my sister."

"Yes. Do something for someone else for a change," Arthur snarled. "Go see your sister."

Chapter 15

For two weeks, Arthur remained at Morgan's side. He talked to her, read to her, and combed her hair. He bathed her, changed her sheets and bedclothes. He kept a close watch on her condition and wouldn't allow anyone else to care for her. He administered her medication and held daily conferences with her doctor.

He sat on the side of her bed and took her by the hand. "Baby, can you hear me?"

The thick, ribbed tube protruded from Morgan's esophagus to the respirator beside her bed. Her chest heaved, unable to breathe on her own, as the heart monitor held a steady beep.

Arthur lowered his head and closed his eyes. "Mo, if you can hear me...I love you. I need you here with me. I can't do this alone. I can't live my life without you." He raised his head, leaned forward, and kissed her on the cheek. "Franklin looks just like you." He smiled as he wiped the stream of tears from his face. "I'd like to call him Frank."

Arthur snapped his head around quickly at the sound of the opening door. "What are you doing here?" he snapped angrily.

"I didn't know I needed your permission to visit my sister." Arthur was about to protest her visit before she held up her hand, not in the mood for his shit. "This is not the time." Arthur ignored her and returned his attention back to Morgan. "Any change?" He slowly shook his head from side to side.

Raven slowly walked toward Morgan. At the foot of the bed, she grabbed her toes and squeezed them. "Hey, Sis, it's me." She chuckled lightly and said, "Whorina." Raven's hand traced up Morgan's blanket-covered leg and stopped at the tips of her fingers. The stillness of Morgan's fingers sent chills throughout her. She closed her eyes and shook off the chill. "Girl, look at your hair."

Arthur shot Raven a cold, deadly stare. His light complexion turned crimson as his ears warmed. "What's wrong with her hair?"

Arthur combed Morgan's hair every day and did not appreciate Raven's comment. Besides, the sight of Raven made him sick to his stomach.

Raven refused to give Arthur an argument. However, if he continued to be an ass, she would have to oblige him. She ignored him and sat on the edge of the bed.

"Don't sit there!"

Raven relaxed her posture and took a deep sigh. "What's wrong with you, sweetie?" Her tone was sharp and condescending. "It's not my fault she's in here."

Arthur's hazel eyes turned bloodshot. He fixed his lips and snarled under his breath, "You bitch!"

Raven stood to her feet. "All right, let's get this over with right now." She looked down at Morgan. "She can't hear us, so let's hash this out now. You are getting on my last nerve, Arthur."

"My problem is you!"

"Arthur, I've done nothing to you."

Arthur stood erect and balled his fist. He wanted to knock the mess out of her, but he knew better. He surely wasn't crazy. He was well aware of Raven's backlash.

Arthur laughed profusely. "You know, Raven, you crack me up!"

"Lower your voice," she whispered.

"Why? Like you said, she can't hear us."

Raven shifted her weight, folded her arms across her chest, and shook her head in annoyance. "This is so childish."

"I guess you sleeping with your sister's husband ain't childish."

A smile formed at the corner of her mouth. "Yes, well, you are a good lover. That's one thing Morgan didn't lie about."

"You disgust me! You blackmailed me."

"I didn't force you to do anything you didn't want to do."

"Trust me. I didn't want to be intimate with you!" Arthur lowered his shoulders in exhaustion. He was tired of fighting a losing game. "No more, Raven!"

She propped her hands on her hips, jutted out her D-cup breasts, and stuck out her right leg. "I don't know why you're acting as though you are the victim."

"You started this whole charade. What about Chas? Don't you feel like crap messing around on a man who loves your life?"

"On the contrary, you cheating ass dog, you started it when you went out with another woman. And don't you worry about Chas. I take care of Chas just fine. Just as I take care of you." She smiled wickedly.

"Lower your voice," he snapped in a hush tone. His eyes flashed toward Morgan. "She might hear you."

Raven nonchalantly tossed her hand toward Morgan. "She ain't studying us. Besides, she can't hear us. She's in a coma. Remember?'"

At the sound of Raven's voice, Morgan's finger slightly budged. Her eyelids began to flicker uncontrollably. Her lips flinched.

Arthur waved his white flag and conceded. "I can't do this anymore."

Raven stroked her tongue across her lush red lips. "You're not strong enough to avoid me." A smile formed at the corner of her pouting mouth. "You love making love to me."

"No, I don't!"

"Yes, you do. You love sexing me because I do what Morgan won't do."

"Shut up," he whispered, his eyes darting from Raven to Morgan, not noticing Morgan slightly coming around.

Raven walked toward Arthur and placed her hand flat against his chest. "Are you sure you want to give this up?" she teased.

Arthur turned his head away from her, inhaled deeply, and drew his jaws tightly together.

Raven moved in closer and purred. "Don't be so mean, baby." She slid her hand from his chest, down toward his abdomen, and comfortably nestled between his legs. His bulge filled her hand as she caressed him gently. "You love what I do with this." Raven dropped to her knees and looked up at Arthur. "Tell me you don't want me to. Tell me, and I won't."

Arthur looked down at her. He studied her for a few moments before unzipping his trousers.

Raven grabbed hold of his trousers and slowly pulled them down around his knees. She caressed his thighs with her moist lips.

Arthur released a slight moan.

"Tell me you don't want it," she softly spoke, stroking his legs and inner thigh.

Arthur relaxed his body and palmed the back of her head. The look on his face changed from rage to desire. For a split second, he felt the urge to fill her throat with his cream. "Swallow," he whispered.

Raven obliged him and lowered his pants from his knees to the floor. His buttocks filled the palm of her hands as she stroked between his cheeks with her finger. As she took his hardness into her mouth, her finger eased in and out of his rectum.

Arthur's head tilted back and his mouth slowly opened. He moaned deeply and whispered, "Take it all," as he pushed himself to the back of her throat. He shuddered as her tonsils tickled the tip of his manhood.

Raven slowly maneuvered her lips around the shaft, her tongue concentrating on the head, flickering from side to side and round and round.

Arthur tightened his cheeks and expelled a deep-throated moan. He felt himself nearing climax. He pulled himself from Raven's mouth, pulled her to her feet, and bent her over the chair beside Morgan's bed.

To their unawareness, Morgan slowly opened her eyes. Morgan's eyes were opened wide and startled, as if she had seen a ghost. Unable to speak, Morgan watched as her husband sexually maneuvered her sister in ways he'd never done with her. She watched him stroke her sister from behind. She flinched at the smacking sound as his hand connected with Raven's ass. She shuddered when he inserted his tongue in her rectum and made sucking noises.

Arthur grabbed a clump of Raven's hair and snapped her head back as far as it would go.

"Too tight," Raven cried.

"Oh, don't cry now," he said, his face becoming flushed. Sweat beaded on his forehead as he drove into her with force. His deep, long strokes became quick pounding. "Oh shit," he muffled between clinched teeth. "Oh shit!"

Morgan slowly closed her eyes and turned her head as tears streamed down her face. When she opened her eyes, she saw how her tears matched those of Chas.

Chapter 16

John stood in the mirror and admired his sun-kissed, with a touch of honey, flawless physique when he heard the knock at the front door.

"It's open," he yelled from the top of the stairs.

The door opened with a slight whine. "Sup, man? Are you expecting someone? I can come back later."

"What's up, Chas? Yeah, Deborah is coming over, but it's all good. She's not known for her promptness. Make yourself at home. I'll be down in a second."

John carefully brushed his lightly gray-dusted, close-cropped hair with precision, while Phi Beta Sigma, branding him for life, danced on his iron-pumped bicep. He sprayed Perry Ellis in the air, closed his eyes, and walked into the misty rain of smell-good, allowing it to saturate his masculinity.

When God created John, He broke the mold. His six-foot-one-inch frame commanded respect. Sexy and wanted by all, he was an intellectual who craved mental stimulation and, so far, the women crossing his path desperately failed at giving him what he needed. Sure, he could get pussy anywhere, but he wanted more. He wanted his soul mate, the love of his life, someone who understood him, and someone who knew what made him tick. He wanted someone who could do more than just scribble her digits on a piece of paper. He wanted Deborah.

As he smoothed baby oil gel across his "Ph.D. in Oral Gratification" full lips and took one last glance in the mirror before jogging down the stairs, John thought of all he would do to Deborah once she got there.

"Hey, man, good to see you." John greeted Chas with a brotherly hug and offered him a beer.

"Naw, man, I'm cool."

"What? You're passing up brew? You must have some major shit occupying your mind, baby brother."

Chas rested his forehead in the span of his hand, between the thumb and index finger. His body trembled and heaved from the sobs that had begun to escape him.

John took a seat beside Chas and rested his hand on his shoulder. "What's bothering you, baby brother?"

"Nothing," Chas sobbed uncontrollably.

"All right, well tell me about the nothing that has you so upset."

"Man…" Chas jumped to his feet and swung his fists in the air several times. "I loved her. I can't believe this shit! I loved that woman with all I had."

John didn't utter one word. He'd never seen his brother so upset. He allowed Chas to cry, vent, and swing at nothing before he commented.

Chas gathered himself and took several deep breaths. He looked John in the eye and slowly spoke. "I saw another man fucking my woman." John shook his head and stood to his feet. "And to think, I actually thought the bastard was my friend."

"Ramone? Hell, she'd been fucking Ramone all the while. Don't know why it would surprise you, baby brother."

"Naw, naw, not Ramone. She stopped seeing him when we decided to be exclusive, or so I thought. No, I'm talking about Arthur."

"Who's Arthur?"

"Morgan's husband."

"Who's Morgan? Hell, man, you aren't making any sense to me."

"Morgan is Raven's sister."

John slightly chuckled. "You've got to be shitting me."

"I wish I were."

"Damn, I'm really sorry about all of this, Chas."

Chas took a seat on the sofa, leaned back, and propped his head against the wall, staring up at the ceiling. "You know the fucked up part is Morgan was in the room." John looked confused. "They were having sex in Morgan's hospital room while she laid there comatose. Can you believe that shit?"

John shook his head and said, "The power of the pussy."

"No pussy is worth it."

"Well, what are you going to do?"

"I don't know. I haven't thought that far ahead."

"I would hope you are planning to kick the trick to the curb." Chas shook his head. "Aw, come on, Chas. You can't possibly stay with this woman after the raggedy shit she just pulled."

"I love her."

"It's obvious she doesn't love you."

"Look, you don't know her to be talking about her."

John kicked out his leg, propped his hands on his hips, and gave Chas a long stare. "Don't be a fool, Chas. Hey, I'm crazy about Deborah, but let me catch her ass up in the air and she'll be history. It's one thing to be in love. It's another to be a fool for love."

John was getting pissed and wanted to knock some sense into his brother. But, at the same time, he also understood where Chas was coming from and how he was feeling. John would've done anything for his ex-fiancé, Greta. She was the love of his life, until she satisfied her appetite for other women. He loved her so much, he was willing to accept her alternative lifestyle, but he refused to compete with another woman for his woman.

"Chas, I know how you're feeling. I really do. But, brother, you saw her in the act. What did she say when you caught her?"

"They didn't see me. But, Morgan did. That's what's really bothering me. She woke up just in time."

John shook his head in disbelief. "Man, if Deborah ever did any shit like that…"

Chas stood to his feet and approached John. "Yeah, well, Deborah won't do that. Deborah is nothing like Raven. You've got a good woman, Bro. Don't fuck it up." Chas embraced John and whispered, "Thanks, man. I love you," in his ear.

John wasn't big on the L word. He rarely used it, especially after Greta. For him, love was a four-letter word like shit, fuck, and damn. Everybody used it daily like they used toilet paper – not sincere or genuine. But, coming from his brother, he knew it was both.

"I love you, too, baby brother. It's all good. You'll be fine," John reassured Chas while patting him hard on the back.

Deborah tapped lightly and slowly opened the door. She knew John was leaving the door unlocked for her. It was a practice he started immediately after they met. Once their eyes met, he instantly knew she was the one.

John felt himself getting choked up when he broke his embrace with Chas. "Hey, baby girl," he said, kissing Deborah softly on the lips.

"Hi, baby. Hi, Chas, how are you?"

Chas wiped the tear from his eye. "I'm cool, Deborah. It's good to see you again."

Deborah looked at Chas and then shot a puzzled look at John. "Everything okay?"

John reached behind Deborah and closed the door. "Yeah, everything's fine."

"Yeah, everything's cool. I was just leaving. Check you later, John. Deborah, take care."

Deborah embraced Chas. She could feel that something was wrong. Besides, she knew her man all too well and "issue" was written all over John's face.

"You take care of yourself, Chas." The second the door closed behind Chas, Deborah turned to John. "Spill it."

"There's nothing to spill. Now come here and let me taste those lips."

Deborah leaned back, a smile forming at the corner of her mouth. "I'm trying to have you taste something else," she said, winking with a raised brow.

"Oooh, you nasty girl."

Deborah turned and headed up the stairs toward the bedroom. With the climbing of each step, she took off a piece of clothing and tossed it in the air. She was naked by the time she entered the bedroom.

After following closely behind her, John leaned in the doorway and admired her beauty. He couldn't figure out why Deborah was so particular about her weight. He thought she was the most beautiful creature he'd ever laid eyes on. "Just stunning," he voiced while smiling broadly.

"Oh, cut it out. You know I'm fat."

John pulled off his shirt and tossed it to the side. "Please, don't start that shit again."

"See? You will tell me I look fine because you love me and don't want to hurt me," she said, displaying her little girl pout. He loved it when she pouted. It intensified him wanting her.

John stepped out of his trousers. "Babe, don't fuck up the moment." He walked toward her.

"But, baby. . ."

He took her by the arm and pressed her against the wall, rubbing his front against her back. "Damn, you smell good."

Deborah expelled a slight moan of satisfaction.

John rubbed his hand against her supple cheek and wandered to her crack. He used his finger and worked his way down to her throbbing bud.

Deborah inhaled quickly, purred like a kitten, and stretched her arms above her head, her upper body flat against the wall. She pressed her behind into his abdomen.

While John's tongue explored the back of her neck, her body heaved and her legs opened. He inserted his finger into her playground and explored every inch.

Deborah's pants were short and hard.

John grabbed her by the hip and pulled her back from the wall. He bent her over and she placed her hands flat against the floor, rising up on her toes as he slid inside her.

"Hmmm," he groaned. "Hmmm."

With his hands tightly affixed to her hips, John slid in and out with precision, careful not to miss her G-spot as she purred with every stroke.

"Baby…baby…oh baby…yes!" she cried with pleasure as her knees were weakening. It felt as though he was stroking against a nerve that sent a piercing pain down her legs, causing her to lose her balance. "John, baby, what are you doing?"

"Hush," he demanded.

"My legs can't take it," she whined.

Still inside her, John picked her up and carried her to the bed where she assumed his favorite position.

Deborah laid face down on the bed with her behind tooted up in the air. She stretched out her arms and grabbed hold of the sheets. This was the position she assumed when John was nearing climax. His pounding was quick and rapid, causing her to jerk and snap repeatedly. She held on for dear life.

John rose up on his toes and slid deeper inside her. "Ah yeah, baby, you ready for me?"

"Yes."

He slapped her on the behind. "Are you ready?"

"Yes!"

"Tell me you want it," he ordered.

Deborah rose up on her hands and pushed herself into him. "I want it, baby. I want it!"

"Yeah!" he moaned.

She yelled from deep within. "Give it all to me, Daddy!"

John's face distorted and the slightly gray hairs glistened from the perspiration dancing on his chest. He gripped her waist and shivered as his seeds shot from his waist and into the woman he loved more than anything. However, the past would not allow him to tell her so.

Chapter 17

Chas sat outside of John's house and called Raven on her cell phone. He didn't know what he was going to do. Well, he knew the right thing to do, but the right thing wasn't what he wanted. He loved Raven and wasn't sure he could handle losing her.

"Damn, that was some fucked up shit, Raven," he mumbled. "And your sister's husband of all people."

Chas hung up before Raven could answer and slammed his fist against the steering wheel. The hurtful look in Morgan's eyes continued to haunt him.

He started to feel guilty, almost like a backstabber. *What goes around comes around,* he thought. Karma is a motherfucker, and it was his turn to be on the receiving end. He had taken Ramone's lady, and now she was giving her love to someone else.

Speaking of the devil, where was Ramone? Chas hadn't seen his best friend in days. He called Ramone on his cell phone and got no answer. He dialed his home number and there was no answer. He'd decided to leave a message, but the mailbox was full.

"He must have a new piece of ass," he mumbled.

After thirty minutes of contemplation, Chas shifted his car into reverse and backed out of the driveway, heading in the direction of the hospital. He needed to see Morgan.

Chapter 18

Deborah stood before the window in all of her splendor. Despite what she thought of herself, she was an attractive woman with a sexy personality and John loved every inch of her. Of all the men she'd dated, only John made her feel comfortable enough to stand before him unclothed and with confidence.

Deborah folded her arms across her chest and peered out the window. "What's going on with Chas?"

John crawled beneath the sheets, fluffed the pillow beneath his head, and collapsed. "What do you mean?" He folded his hands behind his head and stared up at the ceiling.

"Don't play stupid, John."

"I'm not."

"Then answer the question."

"I did."

Deborah faced John, sighed deeply, and dropped her hands to her side. "I hate when you do that."

"Do what?"

"Play word games with me. What were you and Chas talking about before I came in?"

"It's between me and my brother."

"Go ahead, keep your secrets," she pouted. She was doing it again. She knew how to make John conform to her demands.

John sat up and patted the edge of the bed. "Come here, you spoiled ass brat," he chuckled.

"I am not."

"You are too."

Deborah sat on the edge of the bed and leaned in to John's face. "You know I love you," she mused. John stroked her cheek. "You still won't tell me?" she continued pouting.

John smiled and kissed her soft, pouting lips. Deborah warmly welcomed his kiss as her tongue played with his. John wrapped his arms around her neck and pulled her down with him on the bed. Their passionate kissing turned into a rodeo as Deborah straddled her stallion, grabbed tight to his triceps, and rode him to the finish line. John's toes curled tightly and his arms stretched high above his head. The muscles in his body flexed each time she gripped her muscles tightly around his member.

John tried to maintain, but Deborah was draining him. "Damn, girl!"

A smile formed on her face. She knew she had him at his weakest point. Her pace quickened.

John grabbed on to her hips. "Slow down." Deborah ignored his request. She became possessed. "Baby, slow your roll," he pleaded. She moved faster and faster. She leaned into him and gripped him around the neck. "Deborah!" She shook her head from side to side as her grip tightened. John wrapped his hands around her wrists. "Deborah," he cried as he felt his passageway slowly closing, causing him to lose oxygen. His head was spinning. He closed his eyes to keep from losing it. He called out to her once more before bashing her upside the head with his fist, knocking her off of him and onto the floor. He rose up and grabbed himself around the neck. "What the fuck is wrong with you?" he coughed. Deborah laid on the floor in a fetal position, crying.

"What was that, Deborah?" Deborah continued crying. "Baby, why did you spaz out on me?" John questioned. After two years, he thought he knew his woman.

"I don't know," she whispered through sobs. "I got carried away. Something in me... I don't know, baby."

Deborah sat upright and reached out for the man she had loved for so long. There was nothing she wouldn't do for him. John gave Deborah the world. Despite his hesitancy, he felt she deserved to be loved in a way she'd never been loved before. Besides, she never took his love or his gifts for granted.

Still in shock at what had taken place, he didn't know whether to go to her or run for his life. He'd been with women who were violent and vowed to never venture down that road again. But, Deborah was different. She never exhibited a mean bone in her body, which is why her actions had scared him.

"John, baby, please," she cried. "Don't stop loving me."

Her words moved him toward her. "Deborah, I could never stop loving you." He knelt down before her. "However, I am concerned with your behavior. I've never seen you like this before. Was it something I did to provoke your behavior?"

Deborah cradled herself under his shoulder. "Just hold me," she whimpered.

John held her close and slowly rocked her. He knew how to soothe her. He hummed her favorite tune, *Feel the Fire*. Deborah loved Peabo Bryson, and John made it a point to never have her miss any of his concerts, even if it meant flying from city to city.

While rocking her, Deborah buried her face in his chest and whispered, "Baby, I love you. You do know that, right?"

"I know you do, baby girl."

Deborah dozed off in his arms as he tried to make sense of the recent event.

Chapter 19

It had been a long day.

Raven wiggled her toes in the water and tested the temperature before slipping out of her robe and emerging herself in a mound of lush white bubbles. She flipped the switch on the portable whirlpool and sighed deeply as the jet stream swirled water and bubbles about the tub, relaxing her. She leaned her head back against the marigold-colored tile wall and reminisced on her escapade with Arthur. A smile formed on her face. Then, in an instant, it was gone. She felt her heart drop at the thought of her inexcusable actions for that day. She was happy Morgan was unable to witness her despicable act.

She slid down further into the tub, sighed deeply, and closed her eyes. She wished she had a joint. Mental pictures of Arthur drilling into her sent chills through her. She couldn't understand what was so bad about loving Morgan's husband. After all, they were sisters and always shared things. Why not share a husband?

It was Morgan's fault she was having an affair with Arthur anyway. Had Morgan not discussed her and Arthur's lovemaking, she would not have wanted to sample the goods for herself. One thing Raven learned a long time ago was to never share bedroom secrets with another woman, because when you least expect it, when you're not in your bed, the other woman will be, sampling your goods. She thought it to be a shame Morgan hadn't learned that lesson as well.

Raven raised her bubble-covered leg and extended it in the air. She softly ran her fingers from her calf muscle to her inner thigh, toward her peach where she inserted one finger. She played around wanting to feel what Arthur felt whenever he was stroking inside her. Her insides felt like softly padded walls. She often wondered what it felt like to be inside of a woman. She had her opportunity with Marcy, but the dildo really didn't give her much of an idea as to what it felt like to be inside, only on top. Although she enjoyed herself immensely with Marcy, she felt jilted. However, she was thankful to Marcy for introducing her to the wonderful world of dildos.

Marcy was a weak woman and I'll never be weak, she thought. She shook off the thoughts of Marcy and turned her focus to Chas. She felt awful for giving Chas' stuff to Arthur. Still, she didn't have a problem with splitting her time between them evenly.

Raven cared deeply for Chas, but she could never be a one man woman. It wasn't her style. Besides, she tried the one-man woman stuff with Ramone and look at where it got him ¯ pushing up daisies.

Raven pulled herself from the bath. She never stayed in long enough for her skin to wrinkle, just long enough for her to relax and erase all guilt she felt. She stepped out of the tub, reached for the soft pink over-sized towel, and wrapped it around her. Wet footprints followed her to the bedroom where she removed her silver bullet from the nightstand drawer. Thanks to Marcy, she was a regular patron of the Pleasure Chest in Georgetown. Raven was stocked with more sexual paraphernalia than Vanessa Del Rio had porn videos.

She sat down on the bed, spread her legs, and gently massaged her clitoris until she felt it swelling between her fingers. Her head fell back with pleasure as she raised her leg in the air and extended it as far as her muscles would allow. The intensity was building inside her. She lowered herself back on the bed and turned the silver bullet on to level one, a steady pulsating rhythm. Raven cooed and increased to level two. The vibrating hum increased and so did Raven's moaning.

"Umm, right there. Keep it right there," she instructed herself. "Don't stop." She shuddered at the pleasure ripping through her body.

With the blink of an eye, and unable to control the anticipation of one hell of an orgasm, she skipped levels three and four. She pressed the vibrator against her swollen bud, closed her legs tightly, and squeezed her buttocks tight. She couldn't stand it anymore, but she was determined to hold the vibrator on her clitoris long after the orgasm. She was going to try anyway.

Raven felt the urge to urinate. "Let it go, girl," she yelled, cheering herself on. "Don't hold it. You can do it. Let it go. Whoowee!"

She resisted the urge to hold back the urine and allowed it to flow. Her body jilted and her nipples pointed upward.

She turned off the vibrator, tossed it to the side, and lay there staring up at the ceiling. Her phone rung, but she was too far off in La La Land to answer it. She knew it couldn't be Morgan, because she was in a coma. So, she closed her eyes and fell off to sleep.

Chapter 20

Chas' stomach knotted when he entered Morgan's hospital room. The smell of sex continued to linger, overpowering the hospital stench he hated since he was a child and had his tonsils removed. He gathered his composure and crept toward the bed. He gently sat on the bed, took her hand in his, and gently caressed it. Tears welled up in his eyes as he wondered what he would say to her. He felt numb. He felt sick. The whole scene sickened him.

Morgan sighed deeply as she opened her eyes. She gave Chas a piercing look. Her eyes spoke volumes.

"Did you see it?" Morgan nodded her head yes. "Did they know you were watching them?"

Morgan shook her head no. Chas clutched Morgan's hand tighter. "Morgan, I am so sorry. I don't know what to say." Morgan squeezed his hand and closed her eyes tightly, forcing the tears from her ducts. Chas erased her tears with his thumb, in some way hoping it would erase the pain that ached inside her heart. "I came back to check on you. I wanted to make sure you were all right," he said, forcing a smile. Morgan blinked her eyes, unable to speak. Tubes continued to extend from her. "Has the doctor seen you yet?" Morgan shook her head no. "So, they don't know that you are out of your coma."

Morgan's eyes stretched wide open. *Coma, what coma?* she thought. *What is he talking about?*

Chas could see fear dancing in Morgan's eyes. He patted her hand. "Have no worries, Morgan. You're going to be fine. Let me get the nurse, all right?"

Chas returned with the nurse on his heels. She checked out Morgan and rushed to call a doctor. Within minutes, the tubes were removed and Morgan was fine.

After the nurse left, Chas sighed heavily and sat on the edge of Morgan's bed.

"Can you speak now?"

Morgan swallowed, cringing her face. "Water…" she managed to speak, but with much difficulty.

Chas lifted the glass of water to her lips as she sipped. "How are you feeling?"

She swallowed hard and cringed again. The tubes had rubbed her throat raw. She felt like she had her tonsils removed. "What happened to me, Chas?"

"You and Arthur were in a car accident," he answered, frowning.

"He wasn't hurt," she managed to say as she turned her head and stared at the chair where she painfully watched her husband having sex with her sister. Tears made puddles on her cheek.

Chas was tuned into her thoughts. "Don't worry about that now. You have to get yourself better. Hey, guess what?"

"What?"

"You are a mommy," he announced, this time displaying a genuine smile.

Morgan slightly raised her head and looked down at her belly. She smiled and began to cry. "My baby…" she whispered.

"Is all right. Your son is just fine."

Morgan's eyes lit up and sparkled. "I want to see him."

"I don't see why not." Chas reached for the buzzer and buzzed the nurse's station. "Mrs. Carrington would like to see her baby," he spoke into the intercom.

Morgan grabbed at her heart and smiled. Then, her face dropped. Again, she cringed her face as she swallowed. "I don't remember giving birth."

"You had a C-section." Morgan gently patted her stomach and immediately felt the discomfort. She flinched. "You need something for the pain?"

Morgan pursed her lips together and shook her head. "I'm okay."

"I will go now so you can get your rest. Let me know if there is anything you need, all right?"

Morgan smiled and mouthed, "Okay."

Chas leaned down and kissed her on the cheek. "See you later."

Morgan watched the door shut behind Chas. She closed her eyes and cried like a baby. Then, as if someone had smacked her, she gasped turned off the waterworks. She got angry. She pounded her fist against the bed. "Hell hath no fury like a woman scorned," she mouthed. And Morgan was truly scorned.

Chapter 21

"May I have some water?" Morgan licked her dry lips and swallowed deeply as she moved about in her bed. "I feel sore," she said, trying to sit up in the bed.

"Well, you've been out for quite some time, sweetie."

The nurse raised Morgan's head and tilted the chilled cup of ice to her lips.

"Water."

"Sorry, baby, you can't have water just yet. Maybe later." She smiled a sympathetic smile. "Here, put a few chips in your mouth. It's all the same, just solid instead of liquid."

Morgan titled her head back and allowed the melting ice to flow down the back of her throat.

The nurse grabbed Morgan by the wrist and pressed her thumb and index finger firmly around her wrist. She stared at her watch in silence as she checked her pulse.

"When can I go home?"

"Soon, real soon, baby."

Arthur nonchalantly graced the room. Morgan's eyes froze on his lean form. She was conscious of his athletic figure. His muscular arms were bare and his movement toward her bed was swift and full of grace, somewhat smug and cocky. *The cocky bastard*, she thought. *How dare he come in here as if nothing happened?*

"Hey, babe! You look great. How are you feeling?"

Morgan remained silent.

"Oh, she's doing much better," the nurse answered.

He placed his weight on the edge of the bed and rested his hand atop her sheet. Staring straight ahead, Morgan was careful not to let her fingers touch his.

His full lips curled, as if in the form of laughter. "I spoke with Dr. Struthers," he said. "He says your doing fine and can be discharged today, if you feel up to it."

Morgan didn't budge. She wasn't going to. She couldn't believe this man, who she loved more than her own life, had committed the Cardinal Sin against her. Her emotions were reeling out of control, and she found herself responding to him harshly.

"I saw you," she said flatly.

The puzzled look on his face did not confuse her one bit. He felt every bit of her negative energy penetrate deep within him.

She looked toward the nurse and said, "Leave us, please. I need to speak with my…" She looked toward Arthur and rolled her eyes. "My *husband* in private."

The nurse obliged Morgan's request.

Morgan's glare pierced through Arthur. "How could you?" Her tone was sharp this time and on point.

"Honey, what are you talking about?"

Her head jerked toward him, irritated by his mocking tone.

"Yes, I'm ready to go home, Arthur, but not with you!"

He was too startled to be confused. He could feel it in his bones. She knew about Raven. He lowered his head and closed his eyes.

"How did you find out?" he whispered, his insides doing cartwheels.

"All closed eyes aren't asleep." A tear graced his cheek. He stared wordlessly at her, his heart beating at a rapid speed. "How long?" she asked. Arthur shook his head defiantly. He couldn't bring himself to discuss his adultery with his wife. "How long?" she snapped, determined to receive an answer.

"I don't want to lose you, Morgan," he whimpered.

With a slow drawl, she asked again, "How long?"

His shoulders slumped with a heavy sigh. "Not long."

"Why? I need to know why you felt the need to be with another woman, especially my sister!"

Arthur could no longer hold back. He sobbed like a newborn being smacked on the ass. "She made me do it," he whined, his face flushed red and confused. He reached for her.

Morgan jerked from his grasp, shooting him a deranged look. She sat up in the bed and folded her arms across her chest.

"Oh, this is going to be good," she fussed sarcastically.

Arthur stood up, lowered his head, and shoved his hands inside his pants pockets. He stuck out his bottom lip in deep thought and sighed heavily while looking around the private room. The floral print wallpaper was unusual for a hospital room. The matching curtains made him feel like he was standing in the middle of an arboretum, about to be swallowed by a giant man-eating plant. He felt the walls slowly closing in on him.

Morgan's eyes were glued to his face; waiting to see what lie would slip from his lips.

"She blackmailed me."

Morgan dropped her hands in her lap and laughed hysterically. "Blackmailed you?" Morgan's laugh was uncontrollable, almost close to deranged. She pressed her hand against her stomach, trying not to pop her staples. She looked around the room. "I need a mirror." She continued laughing, taking deep breaths between cackles. "I want to see the words 'Boo Boo, the Fool' written across my forehead in big, bold ass letters!"

"Yes, she blackmailed me. You know what your sister is capable of doing," he said. The tone of his voice held a hint of annoyance.

Morgan's laughter seized as she began to tremble. "Yes, I do know," she whispered. "On second thought, Arthur, I don't want to hear your excuse," she retorted in cold sarcasm.

"But, Morgan. . ."

She gritted her teeth and shouted, "No!" She tossed the covers off of her and sprung to her feet. She tilted forward, losing her footing. Arthur rushed to her side and grabbed her by the arm. "Get your hands off of me!" Arthur stepped back and dropped his arms to his side.

"I don't know what to say," he whimpered.

"What excuse could you possibly have for fucking my sister?" she yelled, breathless with rage. She swallowed hard. "I can't believe you did that to me, Arthur," she cried, biting down on her lip until it throbbed. She pressed her hand over her face as her body convulsed from her tears. "Why did it have to be my sister?" She sat on the side of the bed, clasping her hands and resting them in her lap. She lowered her head in defeat. "She takes everything from me," she mumbled. She felt a wretchedness of mind she'd never known before. Her heart ached.

Morgan knew Raven was capable of many things and to what lengths she would go to get what she wanted, but never in her wildest dreams did she think her sister would defile their relationship and commit the ultimate crime against her by sleeping with her husband.

Beads of moisture clung to Arthur's damp forehead. His massive, self-confident presence was now wimpy. He sat on the edge of the bed beside her and stared off into nothing. He inhaled deeply, allowing the disinfectant smell of the hospital room to wrap around his lungs. He closed his eyes and tried his best to pray it all away. But, it was too late. What was done was done. His chest heaved as he tried to find the words, any words, to make things right with her.

Deep down in his soul, Arthur knew there was nothing he could do or say to rectify the mess he had gotten himself in. While Morgan was a loving and caring woman, she was also as stubborn as they come. Nonetheless, he had committed the ultimate sin. He'd betrayed her.

Arthur moistened his dry lips. A muscle flicked angrily at his jaw. "What's the point? You're not going to believe me. You believe nothing when it comes to her."

Her lips parted in surprise. "I believe my eyes, Arthur."

"Baby, I would never. . ."

Morgan raised her hand, cutting off his lie she refused to endure. "I don't want you anymore, Arthur."

"But she made me do it!" he blurted out.

Morgan smiled to herself as she spoke. "Oh I see, she tripped and her mouth landed on your dick. Is that what I'm to believe?" Her mouth took on an unpleasant twist. "No, wait…you tripped and she fell on your dick?" She chuckled at the bullshit he was feeding her.

"I love you," he proclaimed.

She shook her head in disbelief as tears streamed down her cheek. "Just go, Arthur. You don't know the meaning of love. If you did, you wouldn't have screwed my sister in my face."

As the image of Raven on her knees, with her face in his groin, played over and over in her mind like a poorly directed x-rated movie, she darted to the bathroom and dry heaved repeatedly.

Morgan pulled herself away from the porcelain throne and grabbed hold of the sink. Still feeling weak, she leaned against the cold steel sink and slowly raised her head, peering at the vision in the mirror and not recognizing the woman before her. It was the first time she'd looked at herself since the accident. She looked tired, worn and scarred. With her index finger, she traced the ugly, bruised abrasion from the corner of her eye, down over her cheek, to her jawbone. She ran her fingers through her coarse hair. Her hair badly needed to be relaxed. She slowly released the sink and took a step backward. She looked and felt one dress size smaller. She grabbed her stomach and in a fit of panic, she fled from the bathroom, out of her room, and into the hallway toward the nurse's station.

Arthur chased behind her, grabbing at her before she reached the nurse's station. "Morgan, please."

"Get the fuck away from me!" she yelled to the top of her lungs. "Get away! Get away! Get away from me!" she yelled even louder. Out of breath, she could hardly lift her voice above a whisper. Morgan clutched tightly to the desk and lowered her head. "My baby, where is my baby? I asked for him hours ago."

The nurse rushed toward Morgan and grabbed her just in time as she collapsed in her arms. "I need some help, please!" the nurse yelled out.

Nurses rushed from several patients' rooms and assisted Morgan to her room.

"I want to see my baby," she spoke softly and in a daze.

"Mrs. Carrington, we need you to get back in bed." The hospital staff lifted her into the bed, covered her, and lowered the head of the bed.

"I want my baby," Morgan cried.

"We'll get your baby to you right away," one nurse said as they all departed from her room. Morgan rolled over onto her side and sobbed. She felt like dying.

"Morgan," Arthur whispered from across the room.

"Leave me alone, please, Arthur. Just go."

Hours had passed and the sun had set. The full moon shone through the opened blinds as the door slowly opened. Morgan raised her head and shielded her eyes from the blinding light. After her episode at the nurse's station earlier, Dr. Struthers had decided it was best for her to reside at Washington Hospital Center one more day.

"Here he is," the nurse announced, smiling as she approached Morgan. "He is such a good baby. He hardly cries at all. We just love him down in the nursery."

For the first time since his birth, Morgan was finally laying eyes on the only one who would never betray her. She reached for him and cradled him in her arms while stroking his cottony soft cheek with her nose. She looked down at his wrist where 'Baby Carrington' was inscribed on a plastic bracelet.

"Hi, Franklin," she whispered in his ear, choking on her tears. It'd been days since she'd given birth and she was seeing her child for the first time. She thought back to her dream and smiled. "You're named Franklin Ward Carrington after your grandfather," she whispered into his delicate ear. "You're beautiful." Displaying a proud, motherly smile, she slid down in the bed, held Franklin close, and drifted off to sleep.

Chapter 22

Parking at Tradewinds on Thursdays for happy hour was like FedEx Field on Sundays. Mercedes Benz, BMW, Cadillac, Lincoln, and every other brand name vehicle lined Allentown Way, spit-shined and all. This was definitely an old school crowd. Classy black folk, dressed from head to toe in the latest fashion trends to pimp attire, embarked upon Tradewinds like flies.

When Raven entered the foyer of the club, she didn't know whether to take the stairs up to the second level dance floor or enter the dance floor to the right. She took one step forward and peeped to her right, spotting Jo and Dora holding stools at the bar. She took a deep breath and walked in their direction. Raven was never one to do the club scene, so this seemed quite new to her, especially when it came to partying with folks much older than her, even though she could be partial to older men from time to time.

The club was packed and The Temptations was asking, "Who wants to be like the Joneses?"

Raven walked up behind Jo and tapped her on the shoulder. "Hey, girl," she smiled.

"Hey, Raven. I didn't think you were going to make it."

Dora looked over her shoulder and shot Raven a snide look. "You're lucky we were able to save you a seat." She removed her purse from the empty barstool beside her. "It's packed in here tonight."

"You're too kind," Raven retorted.

"Ray, what're you drinking?" Jo asked, motioning for Coco, the bartender. "Girl, Coco's drinks will surely knock you on your ass, so make sure you order a mild drink because she makes them strong."

"I heard that," Coco said, approaching the group of women. "My drinks aren't strong. They're just good," she laughed. "What can I get you?"

"I'll have an Orgasm," Raven ordered.

"Regular or multiple?" Coco asked.

"What's the difference?" Jo inquired.

"The difference is if you only have one orgasm, then your man can't fuck," Sharon interjected with laughter.

"Hey, girl, you're late." Jo smiled as she gave Sharon a sisterly embrace.

"I know. I started not to come." Sharon hopped up on the stool beside Jo and leaned forward, looking past Jo toward Dora. "Hi, Dora."

Dora turned toward Sharon and smirked. "Hi."

Jo elbowed Dora and then offered to buy Sharon a drink. "Don't pay grouchy no mind."

"Jo, I told you about calling me grouchy. I'm not grouchy."

"Oh hush, grouchy," Jo teased.

Dora rolled her eyes and turned her attention to her drink. "I feel like dancing," she volunteered loudly, in hopes the man sitting nearby would ask her to dance. She jerked her shoulders to the beat of the music, trying to get his attention. The girls chuckled at her and commented through whispers and laughter. Annoyed, Dora hopped off her stool and asked, "Who's ordering chicken wings?"

Sharon chuckled. "I was wondering the same thing."

Raven sat quietly on her stool, looking around and wondering what the hell she was doing partying with people twice her age. As she sipped her Orgasm, an ebony sister stood beside her between the two barstools, trying to get Coco's attention.

"Excuse me," the woman called out to Coco. "Can I get a drink please?" Annoyed, the woman mumbled under her breath, "damn," and opened her purse. "I go through this every Thursday with her ass," she fussed. "I swear, she gets on my nerves, prancing around and shit, but she does make the bomb drinks, though." Raven attempted to ignore the woman, but she wasn't having it. "What're you drinking?" she asked Raven.

Raven smiled and rolled her eyes upward. Obviously, she wasn't in the mood to converse with someone she didn't know from a can of paint, especially not this chunky monkey. Raven made it a point to surround herself with women who didn't cause her to stand out, but rather enhanced her. "An Orgasm, Multiple Screams, or something like that."

"Oh, I see," the woman said. "It looks like a White Russian or a Kaluah and cream."

Raven nodded in agreement. "It tastes like one, too."

They both chuckled when Coco approached them. "What can I get you?"

The woman said, "Absolut and cranberry juice."

"Coming up!" Coco sang, obviously having tasted too many stirrers.

Cocoa retrieved a glass, filled it with ice, and pulled the Absolut vodka from the back shelf, complete with top shelf liquor. She poured the vodka halfway full in the glass and topped it off with a splash of cranberry juice.

"Damn," the woman mumbled loudly to herself.

Coco smiled, stirred the drink with a stirrer, and then swiped the stirrer across her tongue to make sure the drink was on point. "Whew! Enjoy it, girlfriend. I guarantee you won't need another one."

The woman took a sip and turned up her face. She swallowed hard, opened her mouth, and began fanning her tongue, as if putting out a fire. "Straight vodka!"

"Just the way I like it," Coco sang as she took off to the end of the bar to serve the next recipient who was sure to be knocked on their ass, too.

"My name is Cassie," the woman said to Raven.

"Raven, nice to meet you."

At first, the name didn't register. But, like a bolt of lightening striking a tree, Raven jolted and glared at Cassie.

"Something wrong?"

"No, not at all. My drink is a little too strong for me, too," she lied.

Cassie chuckled and asked, "Do you come here all the time? I don't remember seeing you before."

"This is my first time. I doubt if I come again, though."

"Oh, you'll be back. It's easy to get hooked."

Raven shrugged her shoulders. "Yeah, I guess." She took another sip of her Orgasm. "What about you?"

"Yes, I'm a regular. Now, I can't hand dance a lick, but I enjoy the 'fellowship' for lack of a better word," she chuckled. "But," she lowered her head, "I haven't been here for the last few weeks." A tear fell from her eye onto the bar. Raven noticed it immediately.

"Are you all right?"

"I lost someone very dear to me to a suicide."

Raven's eyes bucked out, and Dora's ears grew like Dumbo the Elephant. Raven turned her back to Dora. "Oh, wow, I'm sorry to hear that."

"Thanks, but it's all good. Marcy wasn't a strong woman and it didn't take much to send her over the edge."

"Marcy?" Dora inquired. "Marcy Douglas?"

Cassie's face lit up. "Yes, did you know Marcy?"

"We worked with her."

"Damn, what a small world we live in," Cassie said.

Jo looked at Dora in annoyance and whispered, "Why don't you mind your damn business?"

Dora ignored Jo and continued, "Yes, she and Raven were very tight."

"Really?" Cassie cried. "It's a pleasure to meet people who knew my Marcy."

Raven felt like wrapping her hands around Dora's neck and twisting until her head popped off her shoulders.

"We weren't tight. We were co-workers."

"Well, didn't y'all…" Dora flinched. "Ouch, Jo!"

Jo had her fingers around Dora's arm. "Stop starting shit, Dora," she whispered in her ear. "Leave it alone. It ain't any of your business."

Dora snatched her purse from the bar and sauntered off.

Jo pulled a cigarette from her purse and reached for the matches sitting in the ashtray before her. "She is so damn dramatic, I swear."

"Raven, I would love to get together some time and chat about Marcy. I mean, I didn't know of her work side and," she lowered her head, "I miss her so much."

Raven wasn't sure how she wanted to proceed. But, she knew she wasn't finished either, especially with Jay Dawson. He had more than just dealing with Marcy's demise coming to him. If she recalled correctly, Marcy and Cassie were lovers, as well as Jay and Marcy and Jay and Cassie. *This whore gets around,* she thought.

Raven smiled at Cassie and said, "Sure, I'd love to hook up. Maybe we can do dinner."

"Great!" Cassie dug into her purse, pulled out her wallet, and retrieved a business card. "Here is my card. You can reach me at the office or on my cell."

"Great!" Raven mimicked. "I'll give you a call."

Cassie reached for Raven and wrapped her arms around her neck, giving her a warm embrace. "I'm so glad I've met you," she whispered into her ear. Cassie stroked Raven's back as her hand moved slowly toward her waist. "You and I are going to be good friends." Cassie allowed her full lips to brush against Raven's neck. "Call me," she said as she sauntered away.

Raven didn't know how to react and Jo's eyes were plastered on the scene that took place in her face.

"What the hell?" Jo exclaimed.

"A girl isn't safe anywhere, huh?"

"Naw, I guess not. Well, at least you did get hit on, so it ain't all that bad here, huh?"

Raven laughed with Jo. However, in the back of her mind, she was plotting her next escapade of revenge.

Chapter 23

Deborah hopped up and rushed to the front door.

"Hey, Deborah," Chas greeted, giving her a warm embrace. "It's good to see you again. Is John around?"

"Nope, he went to the liquor store."

"Yeah? Hope I'm not about to interrupt anything."

"Nothing that can't wait. Have a seat and chat with me for a minute."

Deborah had always been fond of Chas and felt his choice of women left a lot to be desired. "How are you, Chas?"

"I'm doing good," he smiled, twiddling his thumbs. John had told him how persistent Deborah could be, and he wasn't prepared to deal with her persistency. "I'm doing *real* good."

"No, you're not."

"Excuse me."

"I can see it in your eyes, Chas. You're torn up inside."

"No, Deborah. I'm just fine."

"How can you be? Look, John told me everything, and I think it's terrible what Raven did to you. Hell, it's fucked up what she did to her sister, of all folks to fuck over."

"Yeah, well, thanks, Deborah, for your concern, but I really don't want to talk about it."

"If you don't talk about it, then you'll go crazy. You know I have my master's in Psychology."

"I don't need a psychologist."

"You're in denial."

Chas released a heavy sigh and rested his head in the palms of his hands.

"Okay, fine. But, if you ever need to talk, you know where to find me."

Chas stood and shoved his hands in his pants pockets. "Thanks! I do appreciate you for wanting to help a brother out. But, I'm doing just fine. Let John know I was by, will ya?"

"Sure, I will. He'll be disappointed he missed you. You know how he loves his baby brother."

Chas smiled, nodded, and left. He would've stayed and waited for John, but Deborah was seriously getting up under his skin and he wasn't in the mood to be psychoanalyzed by a broke down, wannabe psychologist.

Chapter 24

Morgan collapsed on the sofa with Franklin nestled in her arm.

After Dr. Struthers signed her release papers, she refused to wait for Arthur. She told the nurse her husband was on his way. But in fact, Arthur had no idea she was being released. It was hospital policy that all patients were escorted out of the hospital via wheelchair and picked up by family or friend. As far as Morgan was concerned, all those she loved were nothing more than dog doo on the bottom of her shoe, and the only one she could trust and depend on was her baby, Franklin. And he wasn't old enough to drive her home. So, she raised hell with the hospital staff and hailed down a taxi.

She looked down at Franklin and smiled. What she was feeling at the moment was indescribable. However, instantly she became sad at the thought of the number of times she'd toyed around with the idea of aborting her baby. Deep down, she was terrified of becoming a mother. She felt like she didn't know how to be a mother. From the looks of Raven, she didn't do such a good job trying to rear her, although she was a mere child herself when their parents died in a car accident.

Morgan envied Franklin's serene and peaceful demeanor. Not a care in the world. She wanted to feel that way, too. She remembered feeling that way once with Arthur. Now, thanks to Raven, that part of her life was over.

She leaned her head back against the sofa and sighed heavily. Just then, the phone rang. She laid Franklin on the sofa and reached for the phone on the end table.

"Yes?"

"What are you doing home? I came to the hospital and they said you had been discharged. Why didn't you call me?"

The sound of Raven's voice made her skin crawl. "I don't feel like talking right now, Raven."

"Okay, you don't have to talk now. I'm coming over."

"No, I'm not feeling up to company."

"Girl," she chuckled, "I ain't company. I'm family. Are you hungry? Do you need me to stop off and pick up something?"

Raven's million and one questions were slowly, but surely, pushing Morgan to the edge. "Raven, please! I'm exhausted and all I want to do is nap."

"Nap? You've been napping for days. Girl, you were in a coma for the longest. Now, I'm coming over. Plus, I want to see my nephew and godson."

Morgan cringed at the thought of Raven raising her baby if anything were to happen to her or Arthur. She spoke in a suffocated whisper. "Fine, Raven. Must you always have your way?"

"Dang, who pissed in your fruit loops this morning?"

"I'm tired and not in the mood for company."

"I'm not company. I'm your sister. But if you want to be alone, then fine. I'll keep my black ass home."

"I'd appreciate you for keeping your black ass home." Morgan hung up on Raven, reached for Franklin, and cradled him. She kissed his forehead, leaned her head back, and closed her eyes.

Chapter 25

"What the fuck part of the game is this?" Raven yelled into the receiver, irate because Morgan had hung up on her. "I am going to call her ass back." Raven pressed redial and angrily tapped her fingers against the refrigerator door. "I don't know who she thinks she is, hanging up on me. I can't stand that shit, and she knows it." When Morgan's answering service picked up, Raven slammed the phone in its cradle and stomped out of the kitchen and into the bedroom.

Morgan never disrespected her in such a manner. She was appalled, pissed, and couldn't imagine what the issue could be. Maybe she was tired. After all, Morgan had been through a terrible accident, as well as having to deliver a baby while in a coma. That would make anyone tired and not want to be bothered. But Raven thought she was different. She wasn't just anyone. She was Morgan's sister and there was no reason, in her mind, why Morgan should be so nasty toward her.

"She's just tired," Raven concluded as she plopped down on her bed. She fell back and stared up at the ceiling. She was bored and felt like getting into something. But what she could get into, she hadn't a clue. She wasn't feeling the club scene. She stretched her arms out beside her and balled a clump of sheets into a fist. She sighed heavily and thought about Chas. She wondered why she hadn't heard from him in a few days. It wasn't like him not to call her, at least once a day. She'd been so wrapped up in Arthur; she'd forgotten to call Chas.

She rolled over onto her side and reached for the phone. The more she thought about Chas, the more she wanted to release some tension. After the third ring, she became discouraged.

Hey, this is Chas. Leave a message. Beep.

"Hi, baby. I've missed you. I haven't heard from you. What've you been up to? Call me. I love you." She turned the phone off and tossed it across the room. "Shit!"

She'd thought about ignoring Morgan's plea and showing up anyway. She wanted to see her nephew. She wanted to see what her baby would look like if she were to have one. But, she thought twice about it. She knew Morgan all too well, and when she was in her mood, she knew it was best to leave her alone.

She sat up and looked around the room. *Damn, I'm bored,* she thought. She glanced at the clock radio that sat on the wicker nightstand beside her bed, then reached over and pressed the ON switch. Smokey Robinson's "Quiet Storm" caused a lump in her throat. Thoughts of the incomparable Melvin Lindsey overwhelmed her.

Raven folded her legs beneath her and rested her chin on the fold of her hand. Tears streamed down her face as she reminisced. It was 1992. She and Morgan were doing their homework while listening to the radio. It was then announced that Melvin Lindsey had died. They were too young to understand or feel the impact Melvin's death made on many people. It wasn't until she was an adult that she felt the pain of losing someone she felt she'd known for years. His smooth, mellow voice lulled her to sleep every night as a child. He was an icon who was truly missed.

Raven was feeling herself becoming uptight and tense. She darted for the bathroom and opened a small fabric-covered, beaded box where she kept her stress reliever. She picked a perfectly rolled joint from the box and held it between her fingers. She fished through the box for a book of matches. After returning to her bed, she struck the match as she held the joint between her pressed lips. The fiery blue flame ignited the stress reliever and she inhaled until she felt her lungs tighten. She leaned her head back and slowly opened her throat, allowing the smoke to float down and into her lungs where it tightened, causing her to slightly choke. She finished the doobie and balled herself up into a fetal position while listening to the tunes of Grover Washington.

When the doorbell rang, Raven sluggishly pulled herself from the bedroom and sauntered down the hall to the door.

"Who is it?" she slurred, her eyelids partially closed. She rose up on the tips of her toes and attempted to look through the peephole. "Who is it, I said?"

There was no answer. Figuring it to be some kids playing a prank, she stumbled away from the door and into the kitchen, scratching her behind in the process.

The doorbell rang again. "Who is it?" she turned around and yelled. Again, there was no response. She exhaled a sigh of irritation and cursed under her breath.

Once again, the doorbell rang. She sashayed to the door and flung it open. "I said…" She stopped abruptly. There was no one there. She looked to the right, then to the left. Nothing. She looked down and there was a small package at her feet. She looked around again before reaching down to pick up the small package. She held her ear to the package. She didn't hear any ticking noise, so she looked around again before closing the door and locking it. Then, she gently shook the package as she walked over to the sofa. She sat the package on the coffee table and slowly took a seat. She wondered what it could be. As she unwrapped the package, her hands began to shake profusely. She pulled the top off the box and saw a miniature coffin inside with a card attached that read, "Continue to do unto others before they do unto you and you'll live to regret it."

Raven dropped the box on the floor, pulled her knees into her chest, and cried herself to sleep.

Chapter 26

"She's getting away with it again," Arthur mumbled to himself as he read the Metro section of the *Washington Post*. He jumped to his feet and slid the chair across the floor with his calf muscles. "Damn! I don't believe this," he yelled. Arthur stared at the article's lead, *"Police are stumped."* The cell phone vibrated on his hip. "Yeah," he answered.

"Did you see today's paper?"

"I saw it," he growled. "I can't believe you got away with it…again."

"I don't appreciate your accusation, Arthur. The dumb bitch committed suicide. I didn't have control over it."

Arthur grunted. "What do you want?"

"Is Morgan home?"

"No, she went shopping."

"Without calling me?"

"I guess she didn't want to go shopping with you."

Raven sighed heavily. "I'm on my way over."

"Why?"

"Because I'm horny."

"Call Chas."

"I don't feel like Chas. I want you. See you in a few."

"The baby is here!"

"Perfect! He's damn near grown and I haven't seen him yet."

Raven chuckled and hung up the phone.

Chapter 27

"What is she doing here?"

Raven's car was parked in the driveway, as if she was the woman of the house. Arthur never parked in the driveway, always leaving way for Morgan.

Morgan slid her key into the keyhole and slowly unlocked the front door. As quietly as she could, she slowly pushed open the door and tiptoed into the foyer. She stood still and looked around. She listened intently, trying to hear something out of the ordinary. All she heard was the quick pounding of her heart. She sat her purse on the marble top table positioned against the wall in the foyer. She slipped out of her shoes and proceeded across the black and white linoleum floor to the staircase in her bare feet. Gently, she tested each step with the ball of her foot, careful not to make a noise. When she reached the top landing, she took a deep breath and gathered her composure. She was sick and tired of Raven and Arthur playing on her intelligence. As she approached the bedroom door, a soft moan from the other side of the door wrapped around her, breaking her heart once again. She gently wrapped her hand around the doorknob and gently turned. As the door slowly opened, Morgan clasped her hand over her mouth. She couldn't move. She quietly watched while her husband loved her sister in front of her face, once again.

Raven's legs were tightly wrapped around Arthur's waist. His pounding was fast and furious. Her moans and groans knotted Morgan's stomach.

"Oooh, yes…" Raven moaned. "Ahh…damn, baby!"

"You like this dick, don't you?"

"Yes!"

Morgan was floored. She'd never heard Arthur speak with such vulgarity.

"That's why you keep coming back!" he said.

"Yes!"

"Here I come!"

"Cum in me, Arthur. Don't pull out! I want your baby, too!"

That was it. Morgan couldn't take anymore. She had seen and heard enough. She knew what she had to do. She backed into the hallway and quietly closed the door. She made her way down the stairs, grabbed her purse and shoes from the foyer, and left the house. Once inside the car, she exploded in gasps and tears. She felt suffocated. Her stomach had turned into a big knot. She opened the car door, leaned out toward the ground, and threw up.

Chapter 28

While the baby slept peacefully in the nursery, Raven stood quietly in the window and watched Morgan drive away. A smile crept across her lips as she folded her arms across her bare chest.

"Hey," Arthur said, standing in the bathroom door, "what has you so fascinated out the window?"

"Oh nothing, just enjoying the beautiful view." She dropped her hands to her side and faced him. "My kitty is still purring."

"Yeah?"

"Yeah." She smiled wickedly. "She needs some attention."

"Like what?"

Raven walked toward Arthur and softly kissed his lips. She bent down and pressed the palms of her hands against her inner thighs.

Arthur looked at her quizzically and asked, "What are you doing?"

"Getting my eagle on." She smiled as she pushed her thighs apart.

Arthur chuckled and inhaled the sweetness wafting from her.

"What are you waiting for?" she asked.

Arthur raised a brow, trying to figure out exactly what she wanted him to do. At times, he thought it difficult to read Raven's mind, which was always farfetched in his opinion.

"Man, lie on your back on the floor so I can sit on your face, damn!"

Arthur shrugged and did as he was told.

"Stick out your tongue," she demanded.

Arthur smiled and thought Raven had the prettiest pussy he'd ever seen. "Be gentle, I don't want you breaking my tongue."

"Shut up," she chuckled as she began to lower herself onto his face.

"Wait!"

"What is it?" she asked, annoyed.

"Spread your lips apart for me."

"You sure are bossy," she chuckled as she used her index fingers to spread open her vaginal lips.

With his index finger, Arthur pulled back the lid over her clitoris and gently stroked it with his tongue.

Raven flinched as her body heaved, her breasts jutting upward. She always thought Arthur was dumb as a box of rocks, but when it came to pleasing her, he did it better than anyone, even Ramone. And Chas couldn't hold a match to Arthur's lovemaking.

Arthur continued to tease her clitoris with his tongue as her body continued to convulse.

Raven pressed her knees against the floor. He grabbed hold of her thighs and held on tight. He sucked her clitoris profusely, bringing her to a full climax. She collapsed to the floor and rested on her side.

"You have to go," he said, bringing himself upright. His erect penis was beckoning for her, but he was running out of time.

She pointed toward his hardness. "Are you sure? Looks like you're ready for a third round."

"Nope, Morgan will be home soon. I can't risk her walking in on us."

"Come to my place then."

"It's tempting, but I can't."

"Yes, you can and you will. Tell Morgan you have rounds tonight. Stay the night with me, Arthur."

Arthur stood with his hands on his hips. "Raven, stop it! Aren't you ever satisfied?"

"We're trying to make a baby, aren't we?" Arthur looked at her dumbfounded. "Then it's settled," she said, looking at the clock. "It's five-thirty. Be at my house around nine-thirty or so."

Arthur stumbled over his thoughts, trying to find the right words. Lately, he seemed to find himself in this predicament – at a loss for words when it came to Raven's demands. He also knew he had to choose the right words. He didn't want to ignite the flame that would light the fuse to the end of the stick of dynamite that stood before him. He was stuck, and he was going to make the best of it.

"I'll see you at ten."

"I said nine-thirty. . ."

"And I said ten. Now take it or leave it!" he snapped.

"Oooh, I like it when you're stern with me, Daddy." Raven slipped into her clothes. "Okay, ten it is. Don't eat. I'll have dinner ready for us."

"What if Morgan cooks dinner?"

"Don't eat it."

"How can I not eat my wife's dinner?"

"You'll figure it out," she said, sashaying out of her sister's bedroom and down the stairs. As she reached the foyer, she bellowed, "I love you and I can't wait to have your baby!"

Arthur sat down on the bed and rested his head in the palm of his hands. What in the hell was he going to do? He was defeated. Mentally, Raven was stronger and, quite honestly, she had his balls in a sling that she could shoot to Morgan whenever the mood struck her. He was in too deep.

Morgan already knew about Arthur and Raven. But what she didn't know about was Reneè, Ramone, and what had happened at the Renaissance. If it were to ever get out that he was an accomplice, he would lose his license to practice medicine and his life would be finished.

In a fit of rage, Arthur punched his fist in mid-air. "I might as well put a gun to my head. My life is over, no thanks to that bitch!"

Chapter 29

Morgan aimlessly wandered around Home Depot until she came across the aisle that housed all pesticides. She only wanted to incapacitate him. She didn't want him dead, because that would've been too good for him. Besides, Franklin needed to have his father. However, she would feel so much better if she could fuck him up the way he fucked her up. And Raven was definitely going to pay for the role, as well. There was one thing Raven seemed to have forgotten. Morgan taught her everything she knows. If it weren't for Morgan, Raven would probably be sitting at the jailhouse. It was because of Morgan that Raven wasn't linked to Marcy's death. Morgan read enough James Patterson novels to know how it's done.

"D-Con," she mumbled. "No other way to fuck up a rat then to feed his ass rat poison. Isn't that right?"

"Excuse me?" a Home Depot shopper said, his voice almost a whisper. "Did you say something?"

"Oh no, I was talking to myself."

He smiled and slowly walked down the aisle, taking a look over his shoulder at her. She had cried so much, the mascara had settled underneath her eyes, making her look like a deranged raccoon.

Morgan felt herself becoming sick. Frantically running about the store, she searched for the bathroom. Once inside the bathroom, she stood before the mirror and gazed at herself. She felt queasy.

She leaned over the sink, turned the water on, and let it run. She reached for a paper towel and held it under the running water, then wrung it out and wiped the hot, sorrowful tear that trickled down her cheek. Her spirits trickled even lower. She gathered her composure, squared her shoulders, and glared at her mirror image. She covered her hair with her hands and squinted critically at her face in the mirror.

"I look like hell," she muttered while wiping the mascara around her eyes, making it worse than it already was. The faucet was still pouring water. She leaned down, splashed water on her face, and then reached for a paper towel to dab the moisture from her face. She gave herself a quick once-over, reached for the door, and stepped out of the bathroom as a woman on a mission. She made a beeline to the pesticide aisle, grabbed two boxes of D-Con, and headed for the register.

"Hello. Looks like we have a rat problem," the cashier donned in a raggedy, scuffed orange smock said, sliding the two boxes of D-Con across the scanner. "That'll be twelve dollars and eight-nine cents," she smiled.

Without a word or show of emotion, Morgan reached into her pocket and handed the woman a twenty-dollar bill. She grabbed the bag and walked away.

"You forgot your change," the cashier called out.

Morgan didn't respond. She held her bag of poison close to her side and kept on strutting, never looking back. She had two rats to take care of, immediately.

Chapter 30

The day had been hot, and the night even hotter. It was Nellie's birthday and Jaspers was filled to the rim for a Tuesday night. Concert attendees had converged on the restaurant after The Budweiser Rhythm & Blues Music Festival had ended at FedEx field.

"The show was off the hook," Nellie shrieked.

"Yeah, it was. What a line-up, too," Jo said as the three divas stood in the foyer of the restaurant, waiting to be seated.

"My panties almost hit the stage, girl, when Teddy started belting out for folks to turn off the lights," Dora chuckled.

"Girl, his wheelchair would've toppled over," Jo laughed.

"Girl, don't be messing with my Teddy. But I'll bet you this one thing. Wheelchair or not, he's still probably fucking like a crazed dog."

Jo and Dora gave each other a high-five as Nellie primped in the smoked, floor-length mirror. "It's crowded in here, y'all. Are you sure you don't want to go somewhere else?"

"Nellie, my feet hurt, and I don't feel like riding all over trying to find something to eat," Jo whined.

"I'm with Jo. Besides, I like the Artichoke Dip here," Dora chimed in.

As they were escorted to a booth in a dark corner of the restaurant, Jo locked eyes with a gentleman having a drink at the bar. She never uttered a word to her girls, which is what she would normally do. This time, she kept him to herself and peered at him through most of dinner.

"Jo, what are you looking at?" Dora asked, looking in the direction of the bar.

"Nothing." "Oh, it's something," Nellie chimed in, followed by her soft, girlish chuckle.

"It's nothing. I want another drink."

"Oh no, Miss Lady, you've got your eyes peeled on that fine brother sitting at the bar," Dora teased.

"Where, where?"

"Over there," Dora pointed, "in the black crewneck top."

"Oh, he's cute, Jo. He smells good, too," Nellie approved.

Jo titled her heard toward Nellie. "Now how do you know he smells good?"

"Because he looks like it."

"Nellie, I think you've had enough to drink, girl," Dora chuckled. "But he does look clean."

"Oh, y'all are silly," Jo said, shaking her head.

"Go over and talk to him," Nellie suggested.

"Huh?" Jo waved her hand toward Nellie. "Oh no, I can't do that."

"Why not?" Dora asked. "You might as well. How many cavities does he have?"

Jo looked at Dora quizzically. "What are you talking about?"

"You've been down his throat since we sat down. If you're interested, go and introduce yourself."

"I don't know…"

"Yeah, Jo, go for it. What do you have to lose?"

"An embarrassing moment," Dora teased.

Jo picked at her food briefly before she decided to make her move. "Fine," she said, tossing her white linen napkin on the table. "Y'all get on my nerves, always daring someone to do something." Standing, Jo straightened her shoulders, smoothed her palms over her fine hips and shapely thighs, and cleared her throat. "Watch and learn."

"Hmm, don't hurt yourself, girlfriend," Dora sung.

Jo strolled about, smiling at a few people as she moved through the crowd. Her steps slowed as she pondered what she was about to do. She wasn't accustomed to approaching men; they always approached her. She tilted her head to one side and stole a slanted look at him. His dress was simple, but rich. She inhaled deeply and wrapped herself in his scent. He was devastatingly handsome. She felt herself moistening. He was making her hot and she was finding it hard to control the urge to jump his bones.

She softly cleared her throat and tapped him on the shoulder. "Hello."

He faced her with his fingers wrapped tightly around his snifter of Cognac. "Hi," he responded, smiling widely.

"May I have a moment of your time?" she nervously stumbled, her ecru cheeks turning terra cotta.

He smiled and extended his hand toward her. "I'm Chas. Would you like a drink?"

"I'm Jo, and a drink would be nice. Thank you."

Chas motioned for the bartender. "Whatever the lady is drinking."

"Cranberry and vodka," Jo ordered, then glanced over her shoulder and smiled at the peanut gallery that kept watch of her every move.

Chas offered Jo his seat and stood close behind her. "So what do I owe the pleasure?"

"Well, umm…"

"Cat got your tongue?" he chuckled.

"No, not at all. I find you very attractive and would like to get to know you."

Chas released an irresistible grin. "You would, huh?"

Jo thought how his dimples reminded her of deep caves. She was tempted to stick her finger inside his cave, but she thought she was already being too forward as it was, and she wasn't going to lead him to believe this was a regular routine with her.

"Will that be a problem?"

His smile widened with his approval. "No problem at all."

"So, Chas, are you single, married, divorce, involved, or widowed?"

"Single, and you?"

"Single, but looking," she replied in a low, sultry voice.

Chas stared at Jo and then burst out laughing. His laughter was deep, warm, and rich.

Jo laughed gently. "What's so funny?" she asked.

"That 'single, but looking' comment was funny. If you're single, of course you're looking," he said.

"Not necessarily. You could be single and not looking for shit."

Chas chuckled, took a sip of his drink, and smiled. "My bad." The smile in his eyes contained a sensuous flame.

Jo smiled and moved in closer. "Could we exchange numbers?"

Chas tilted his head back in thought and pouted his full lips. "Yeah, I'd like that."

After asking the bartender for a pen, she wrote her phone number down on a crumpled white napkin, folded it neatly, and placed it securely in Chas' hand. She leaned in closer and whispered, "Don't wait too long to call me."

He cupped her chin tenderly in his warm hand and pulled her close to him. His breath penetrated her nostrils, leaving her with wet panties. His lips curled into a smile. "Stay by the phone," he whispered as his lips brushed against hers with a feathery swipe.

With weak legs, wet panties, and a shortness of breath, Jo walked through the crowd while trying to maintain her composure.

When Jo returned to the table, Nellie and Dora looked at her quizzically. Beads of perspiration had formed on her top lip. She reached in her purse and pulled out a cigarette.

"Damn, what'd he do to make you need a cigarette," Dora laughed.

"Mmm, Jo, I'm scared of you. Did you get his number?"

Jo nodded her head and inhaled deeply. She held the smoke in and felt it wrap around her lungs. She exhaled and squared her shoulders. "Let's roll." As they walked toward the foyer, Jo looked over her shoulder at Chas. His eyes were plastered on her voluptuous form. "Call me," she mouthed.

Chas smiled, nodded, and downed the remainder of his drink. As Jo sashayed through the doors and into the night, he reached in his pocket and pulled out his cell phone. He unfolded the crumpled napkin and smiled as he dialed the telephone number.

"Your wish is my command," he said in a deep monotone voice that gave her chills from the top of her head to the tips of her chubby toes.

"So I see," she said. "Keep this up and I'll have to give you a treat for being obedient."

"Well then, I'll continue to be good. I want my treat."

Chas hung up the phone and Jo screamed to the top of her lungs.

"Omigosh, what's wrong, Jo?" Nellie asked.

"Girl, I think I have hit the jackpot with this one."

"Who?" Dora asked, noticing how giddy Jo had gotten.

"That was Chas, and you know what?" Jo tucked her cell in her purse and proceeded toward the car. Nellie and Dora followed on her heels. "I'm going to fuck him and it'll be soon, too." The thought of her and Chas entwined excited her and her determination to bed him was even greater.

"That's nasty, Jo. You don't even know him."

"Hush, girl, this is 2004." There was slight amusement in Nellie's tone. "The only thing you need to know is, does he have a condom and was his test results negative or positive."

Jo fell out with laughter.

"Oh my God, Nellie. Let me find out…" Dora started.

"Not hardly," Nellie interrupted. "I'm only saying if she wants to screw the man, then go for it. Shoot, life is too damn short to deny yourself of anything."

"Okay, I agree with that, but being a blatant idiot is a totally different story. Besides, it's not ladylike, and you need to make him work for it. Hell, what ever happened to the chivalry days?"

"They are long gone," Jo smirked.

"Not in my book," Dora groaned, rolling her eyes. "I like to be treated like a lady and not some tramp."

"That's true."

"Make up your mind which direction you're flowing in, Nellie," Jo chuckled. "One minute I should fuck his brains out, the next minute I should be a damn lady."

"Well, let me say this one thing," Dora said. "A man will treat you how you come across. If you come across like a whore, you'll be treated like one. Come across like a woman who has self-respect and demands it, you'll be treated as such."

"Preach on," Nellie cried.

"Shut up, Nellie!" Jo glanced around the packed parking lot. She backed out of the space and pulled forward. As she came to the end of the parking lane, she looked both ways before she looked ahead and saw Chas standing before her. He smiled widely. She smiled widely, too.

"Oh, give me a break," Dora giggled under her breath.

Nellie, who was seated in the back seat, reached forward and popped Dora upside the head. "Leave Jo alone."

"Don't give me a damn headache, Nellie!"

"He is cute, Jo," Nellie smiled. "Roll the window down."

"For what?" Dora asked. "Don't act like you're desperate, Jo."

Jo ignored them and rolled down the window. "Hello, handsome."

Chas approached the shiny black Audi 5000. "Hello, beautiful."

Jo blushed and slightly lowered her head in a bashful manner. "Thank you for the call."

"It was my pleasure. As I said, your wish is my command. Is there anything else I can do for you?"

"Yeah, you can get away from the car so we can go. My feet are killing me," Dora snapped. Nellie popped her upside the head once again. "Damn it, Nellie. Cut that shit out!"

"Don't pay her any mind," Jo smiled in his face. "Can I call you when I get home?"

"Of course." Chas stepped back from the car and shoved his hands into his jacket pockets. "I'll be waiting to hear from you tonight."

Jo rolled up the window and quickly pulled off. "Damn, did you see those teeth?"

"His teeth?" Nellie asked.

"Yeah, girl, his teeth. A man with pretty white teeth will have good smelling breath. I can't stand a man with messed up teeth. Also, it tells me he is up on his hygiene."

"Uh huh, true, but you still need to make him wait," Dora said.

"Yeah," Nellie said. "I agree. If he's a good man, he won't put any pressure on you."

"Damn, y'all, can we have a date first? Geesh!"

Nellie rested her head on the headrest and closed her eyes. Dora kicked off her shoes and rubbed her toes. Jo smiled the entire drive, wondering what she was going to wear on her first date with Chas. And, despite the warnings of her girlfriends, she thought about the cute purple lace ensemble she picked up from Victoria's Secret last summer. Then, it was too small, but it was on sale and she could never pass up a good sale. Now, it fitted perfectly, thanks to the relationship she's had with Weight Watchers all winter long.

Chapter 31

After his vigorous workout at Gold's Gym, Chas soaked in the tub for an hour while the Epsom salt soothed his sore muscles. He'd never been one for soaking in a tub, until after he met Raven. After sex, she had to soak in the tub, and he had to be in the tub with her. She wouldn't have it any other way. He couldn't stand soaking in the tub, but when it came to pleasing the woman he loved, he would go to any lengths, even if it meant sitting in a tub of hot dirty water with after-sex floating around. After dozing off for a moment, he got out, dried off, and slowly pulled on the heavy white terrycloth robe, a birthday gift from Raven.

Chas walked into the kitchen, opened the refrigerator, and grabbed an ice-cold Corona. He searched the refrigerator's crisper compartment for a lime. "I just bought limes," he mumbled, still shuffling through the fridge. Chas' refrigerator definitely needed a good cleaning. In frustration of not finding his lime, he closed the refrigerator and started searching for the can opener. "Shit, I can't find anything in this damn place!" He slammed the drawer closed and used the dishtowel to force the top off of the beer bottle, wrapping his lips around the mouth of the bottle afterwards.

In the living room, Chas plopped down in the Lazy Boy and grabbed the remote from the small wicker table beside the recliner. A knock at the door stopped him from turning on the television. He walked to the door and peeped through the peephole. He leaned back, placed his hands on his hips, and asked, "Who is it?"

"Chas Walker?" came from the deep baritone voice on the other side of the door.

"Who wants to know?"

"Metropolitan Police, sir."

Chas attached the chain and cracked the door. "What can I do for you?"

The officer flashed his badge and then said, "Mr. Walker, we would like to ask you a few questions."

"About?"

"Ramone Jarvis."

"What about him?"

"Mr. Walker, it won't take long."

Reluctantly, Chas removed the chain and opened the door. He couldn't imagine what Ramone had gotten himself into. He opened the door wider and stepped back, allowing the police officers' entry.

"Have a seat."

"Mr. Walker, when was the last time you saw Ramone Jarvis?" the officer asked, ignoring Chas' offer for them to sit.

"It's been a while. Why? Is everything all right?" The officer looked at his partner and raised his brow. "What's going on?"

"Can you give us an exact date when you last saw Mr. Jarvis?"

Chas had become antsy and annoyed at their beating-around-the-bush method. "Look, tell me what is going on or get out of my house," he demanded.

"You don't know?"

"Know what?"

"Mr. and Mrs. Jarvis were found dead."

The harsh lines around Chas' eyes softened. He fell into the recliner and laid his head back. Then, he leaned forward, bowed his head, and remained in an attitude of frozen stillness.

"What relation are you to Mr. Jarvis?"

Chas slowly shook his head as tears welled in his eyes. He spoke slowly. "He is…was my best friend."

"We know this is hard for you, Mr. Walker, but we really need to know if you know of anything that Ramone Jarvis and/or his wife was involved in — drugs, gambling, etc."

His lips puckered with annoyance. He shook his head vigorously. "No, no, no." He held his head in his hands. "Oh my God, who would do this?"

"Sir, you think they were murdered?"

Chas stood to his feet. "Isn't that your job to figure out? They surely wouldn't commit suicide. They had two children, for God sakes!"

The officer pulled out his business card and handed it to Chas. "Please give us a call if you hear or can think of anything at all."

"Yeah, I'll do that," he agreed. He closed the door behind them, sat down on the sofa, and cried for his best friend. He told Ramone over and over, the lifestyle he led would catch up with him soon enough, and it had.

Chapter 32

After Morgan put Franklin down for the night, she walked by the bedroom and Arthur was stretched across the bed, watching television.

"When are you coming to bed, honey?" he asked, bunching the pillow beneath his chin. She paused and nodded her head, not trusting herself to speak. "I'll wait up for you." The tension in her face had increased when she faced him. "Is everything all right, Morgan? You don't look so hot."

"I'm fine. I'm going to get online for a little while," she said in a zombie state.

"Well, don't be too long. It's been a long time since I've had my wife. I miss you, baby." A cold knot formed in her stomach at his declaration. She clinched her hand until her nails entered her palm. "I'll wait up, but don't be too long."

"I won't be long," she managed to say.

In Arthur's office, Morgan sat behind the laptop, signed on, and immediately conducted a Google search for digesting rat poison. Morgan was adamant about doing thorough research. Mind you, she didn't want to kill him. She only wanted to watch him suffer. She wanted him to feel the pain she felt when he and Raven gave her an impromptu porno movie, and then the encore today didn't make things better. She was going to make Arthur pay, one way or the other.

Morgan leaned back in the chair. Glaring at Arthur's cell phone sitting on the desk, she thought about peeking at his address book. Who knows? If he had the balls to screw around with her sister, he would have bigger balls screwing around with a complete stranger. However, she would've preferred a stranger to her sister any day.

She sighed heavily and closed her eyes, napping for a bit before the chirping of Arthur's cell phone startled her. She contemplated answering it, but when it came to his business, she had always minded hers. However, this time was different. She would be kept in the dark no more.

She picked up the phone and looked at the caller ID. It was Raven. Suddenly, it felt like her throat was closing up. She couldn't breathe. The blood rushed through her veins at a rapid pace and sweat began to bead on her nose. She was hot as hell, but couldn't let on that she knew what was going on. Ignoring the ringing phone, she went to bed. She would deal with Raven in due time, one rat at a time.

Morgan slipped under the sheets and turned her back to Arthur. He placed his hand on her hips. "Have I told you how happy I am to have you home?" Morgan cringed. "I really missed you, honey." Arthur moved in closer, spooned her, and kissed her in the crease of her neck. Unable to bear his show of affection, she broke his embrace and moved closer to the edge of the bed. "What's wrong, honey?" Morgan was silent. "Is everything okay?"

"Everything is fine. I'm worn out."

"I guess taking care of the baby is taking its toll on you."

"Yeah, I guess," Morgan replied as Arthur rolled over onto his back and grabbed himself. "What are you doing?"

"Since you aren't going to oblige me, I might as well take care of myself."

"Do what you need to do, Arthur," she snapped.

He sprung up in the bed. "What's that supposed to mean?

"Take care of your business, that's what that's supposed to mean."

"Honey, you must be going through post-pregnancy depression."

"Yes, and so is my twat 'cause you ain't getting any of this tonight, tomorrow night, the next night, or the night after that, you no good bastard!"

"It's over between me and Raven. I promise you I won't touch her again. You do believe me, baby, don't you?"

Morgan ignored Arthur and slid under the sheets further, nestling her head into the pillow. She mumbled a few words and, within minutes, was fast asleep.

Chapter 33

Chas sat quietly as Dr. McKnight studied his test results.

"Everything all right, Doctor? You sure are taking a long time to look over my results," Chas chuckled nervously. He wasn't feeling comfortable with this meeting. As far as he was concerned, anytime a doctor called you in to discuss your test results, it was serious.

"Chas, I'm not going to beat around the bush. When diagnosed and treated in a timely manner, prostate cancer can be healed."

Chas' mouth hit the floor. He felt nauseated and his long easy breaths turned to deep pants. "I have prostate cancer? Are you telling me I'm going to die?"

"Not if I can help it," Dr. McKnight assured.

Chas nodded in disbelief. "How did I get prostate cancer?"

Dr. McKnight removed his glasses from his round face and gently sat them on the desk. He folded his hands and placed his chin in the cradle of his clasped hands. "No one really knows the exact cause of prostate cancer. However, it occurs when new cells in the prostate form when the body does not need them, and old cells do not die when they should. The extra cells form into a tissue mass called a growth or tumor. It can be benign or malignant. Benign tumors are not cancerous and is rarely life threatening. Generally, benign tumors can be removed, and they usually do not grow back. Malignant tumors *are* cancerous and, if not treated early, may be life threatening. Malignant prostate cancer tumors can often be removed, but they may grow back."

"How serious is it?"

"It's centralized. There are various types of treatments we need to discuss, with various side effects…"

"What kind of treatment…surgery, radiation, hormonal therapy? If you can fix it, I'm all for it." Chas dropped his head in the palm of his hands. "Oh God, what did I do to deserve this?"

"Chas, try to stay calm. Getting upset will only hinder your chance of healing. Stay focused on beating this."

Chas tilted his head back as far as it would go and cried. "I don't believe this shit."

"You're not alone. I know exactly how you feel. You can beat this. I am a prostate cancer survivor. But let me tell you something. Before I was diagnosed, my childhood friend was diagnosed. His idiotic doctor informed him that he would probably die of something else before he died of prostate cancer. He kept a watchful eye instead of getting treatment. Two years later, I was a pallbearer, carrying my best friend to his final resting place." Chas clamped his jaw tight and glared at Dr. McKnight. "Now, with that said, there are so many treatment options. We just have to choose the right treatment for you."

Chas inhaled deeply, sat up straight, and squared his shoulders. "You said something about side effects."

"Yes. As with any type of treatment, there are possible side effects. However, everyone is different."

"Well, in general, what are some side effects?"

"Impotence, breast enlargement, depression, nausea, incontinence..."

"What? Are you telling me I'm not going to be able to satisfy a woman?"

"It's possible, but I'm sure you know there are other ways to satisfy a woman besides penetration."

Chas' mouth was tight and grim. "Of course, I do."

"I will have my assistant to give you literature. Read it carefully. Then, you and I will sit down in a few days and go over every treatment option and decide which is best for you, with the least side effects."

Tears welled in Chas' eyes. He felt warm, similar to a female's hot flash. He managed to reply through trembling lips. "I can't believe this. It's like my life is flashing before me."

"Stay positive and let's do what we have to do. Prostate cancer's survival rate is pretty high when treated early. You are in the early stages, but we aren't going to keep a watchful eye. We are going to act appropriately."

Chas shook his head violently, jumped to his feet, and blurted, "Fuck, fuck, fuck!" He swung at nothing and continued punching in mid-air. "Fuck, fuck, fuck!" He dropped down to his knees, panting for air, and broke down into tears, crying like a baby. His face glistened and the whites of his eyes turned crimson. "You know, I thought I had found my soul mate. I thought I had found the woman I would spend the rest of my life with. A couple of weeks ago, I found her fucking her sister's husband." Dr. McKnight stared at him, feeling sorry for Chas' poor soul, but knowing all too well what he was going through. He'd been there and wouldn't wish that on his worst enemy. "Now, I may never find happiness with a woman I can love."

"Chas, you're jumping the gun."

"What woman wants a man who can't get a hard-on?"

"That side effect is a possibility. Like I said, side effects vary from person to person. You may not experience that side effect. Look, let's take it one step at a time. But, I can't have you breaking down on me. Your mental and physical stability has a lot to do with your healing. Do you understand me, Chas?"

Chas nodded his head and grabbed his jacket. "I know what you mean. I'll pick up those pamphlets and schedule an appointment for early next week."

"That'll be fine. In the meantime, if you have any questions, don't hesitate to call me." Dr. McKnight extended his hand. "Deal?"

Chas grabbed his hand and smiled. "Thanks."

Chapter 34

Chas sat on the side of the bed and stared at the floor. For three days, he moped around, feeling sorry for himself and entering the beginning stages of depression. He fell back on the bed and, for an hour, stared at the ceiling as tears streamed down his face and dampened the cotton sheets beneath him. The ringing of the telephone startled him out of his daze. He reached for the phone and dragged it toward him.

"Yeah," he answered.

"Hi, Chas, this is Jo."

His tensed facial expression immediately relaxed at the sound of her voice. He had been conversing with Jo for the past week. He enjoyed talking to her. Jo was well versed in all areas of current events. He loved that about her.

"Hey you, how're you doing?" he asked, a smile forming at the corners of his mouth.

"I'm doing great. Are you busy?"

"No, not busy at all. Kind of glad you called."

"Oh really now?" she flirted. "Why is that?"

"I enjoy talking to you."

"I enjoy talking to you, as well. Do you think we're ready to have a date yet?" she chuckled. "We have been talking for over a week on the phone."

Chas sat up on the bed and stretched his back. "Yeah, I'd like that. What would you like to do?"

"I'm a simple girl. I don't need much. A walk in the park, white water rafting," she chuckled.

"It's a little chilly to be walking in the park tonight, and you can forget about white water rafting. That shit's for white folks."

"Don't act like you've been living under a rock," she laughed. "Black folks will raft down a flowing stream of water in a heartbeat."

"I don't know what kind of black folks you hang around, but the ones I know wouldn't do that shit for nothing in the world," he laughed. He was feeling much better and was out of his state of depression, at least for the time being.

Jo cracked up with laughter. "You are a fool, Mr. Walker."

"Hey, what time is it?"

"Um, it's quarter past six."

"Are you hungry?"

"As a hostage!"

Chas shook his head and smiled. "I've always wanted to dine at the Capitol Grill."

"Ooh, that place is fancy. I hear you can't wear jeans and you have to have a reservation."

"Yes, and it sounds good to me. Want to go?"

"What time?"

"I'll make reservations for nine o'clock and I'll pick you up at eight."

"That sounds good. My address is 292 Fisher Lane. You can pull the directions from MapQuest."

"Okay, will do. See you at eight and dress up. I feel like wining and dining us both tonight!"

Jo let out a slight giggle. "This is going to be fun. I can't wait. I'll see you soon!"

Chas hung up the phone and leapt to his feet. Just what the doctor ordered: a beautiful woman and a wonderful evening of conversation and whatever comes afterwards. Chas rubbed his hands together and headed toward his closet. He flung open the doors, stood back, and contemplated his attire for the evening. It was his intention to enjoy life to the fullest and do everything he'd always wanted to do.

He reached into the closet and pulled out a navy blue blazer, a light blue denim shirt, and beige Dockers. He stretched his clothes out on the bed and then headed for the shower. He stood under the running water, for what seemed like forever, and found a new lease on life. This was a battle he was determined to win.

He turned off the shower, grabbed the towel from the rack on the wall, wrapped it around his waist, and stepped outside of the shower. He stood before the mirror and admired his viral statute. As thoughts of Jo occupied his mind, his soldier rose to attention. He smiled broadly and sprayed on his favorite cologne, Burberry. After dressing, he pulled the directions to Jo's house off the computer and quickly headed toward the door. As he picked up his keys from the table in the foyer, the doorbell rang. Without a thought, he opened the door and came face to face with Raven.

"Hey baby!" she exclaimed, wrapping her arms tightly around his neck. "Oh, you feel so good. You smell good, too. Where are you going?"

"Hello, Raven. I'm going out for awhile," Chas responded flatly.

She pouted her lips. "Shoot, I wanted to spend some time with you."

"Where've you been hiding, Ray? I haven't seen you in a couple of weeks." Irritation grew in his voice.

"Well...I've been helping out Morgan with the baby. You know she's a new mother and doesn't bit more know what she's doing than a man on the moon. But, I took a break because I've been neglecting you, baby."

"Uh huh, check it, Ray. I have somewhere I need to be. Let me get back at you later. Cool?"

Raven took a step backward. "Let you get back to me later? What kind of shit is that?"

Chas leaned in and kissed her on the cheek. He knew she was about to kick off in rare form. "Baby, I'll call you tonight."

"Okay, and I'll come back over. Okay?"

"Yeah, sure, baby."

Chas blew past Raven and darted for his car. He hopped inside, shut the door, and locked it. Raven never took her eyes off of him. Her glare was cold and icy. He started the engine and looked over his shoulder before backing out of the driveway. Raven blew him a kiss and waved goodbye.

"He's up to something," she mumbled. "I don't know what you're up to, Chas, but you can best believe I will find out. You're fucking with the wrong person."

Chapter 35

Jo was a sight for sore eyes as she stood in the doorway, motioning for him to enter. "Did you have problems finding the place?"

"No, not at all. MapQuest made it quite easy to find." He kissed her on the cheek and walked into the foyer. "You have a beautiful home."

"Thank you. Do we have time for a drink?"

Chas looked at his watch and said, "Sure."

"Great. I'm a Crown Royal girl."

"I'll have mine on the rocks."

"Coming right up." Jo disappeared into the kitchen and yelled out, "You sure do look mighty dapper, Mr. Walker. A girl wouldn't mind you on her arm."

"I surely have no complaints with you."

Jo returned with the drinks. "I'd like to make a toast." They raised their glasses upward. "To a wonderful friendship and, if you play your cards right, more than friendship." They clinked their glasses together and then took a sip. Chas leaned in and brushed his lips against hers. He inhaled her scent and smiled. "I love the way you smell."

Jo pointed her finger at him. "Keep that up and we won't make the reservation."

"You can't blame a man for trying, can you?"

"No, a man knows a good woman when he sees one," she cooed, moving in closer. "I've been waiting for this opportunity, Mr. Walker."

"Oh? And what exactly were you waiting to do?"

"This," she said, pressing her lips against his. He inhaled deeply, taking her all in. He broke the embrace and pulled back, glaring at her. Her beauty was traditional. "Lady, why are you alone?"

Jo smiled and stepped away from him. "Darling, I'm not alone. I have myself."

"That is not what I mean, and you know it," he chuckled.

"Yes, I know what you mean. I love being single. I love being with me. I enjoy not having to deal with the drama and hassles that come with a relationship. Now, that's not to say that I will not welcome a relationship into my life. On the contrary…" She took a seat on the sofa and crossed her legs. Her coke bottle-shaped legs caused him to rise like a tray of homemade rolls. Any minute, he would be ready for the oven. She patted the seat beside her. "Sit next to me, Chas."

Chas took the seat and smiled. "Jo, I don't know where we are going to go, or if we are going anywhere at all."

"I thought we were going to the Capitol Grill."

Chas lowered his head and smiled. "We are, but there's something I want to share with you."

"I'm listening."

"I went to see my doctor today, and," he hesitated, paying close attention to her facial expression. He didn't know how to tell the woman he had just met that he may or may not be dying, but he felt he owed her that much before going any further. "He told me I had prostate cancer."

Jo's smile vanished and was replaced with a blank stare. Her vanilla cream cheeks turned strawberry red as her eyes filled with tears and her heart filled with unhappiness for Chas. "Oh, Chas, I am so sorry."

"I thought you needed to know." He took her hand and pulled it close to his lips. "I really enjoy you, Jo, and there's more."

"What more could there possibly be?"

"Before I met you, I was in a relationship."

"Was? How long ago was it, Chas?"

"Uh, well…when we met at Jaspers…"

"Which was about two weeks ago."

"Yes, um, well…how can I say this?"

"I'm sure you'll find a way."

"When I met you, I was still seeing her…"

"Who is she?"

"That's not important."

"Oh, it's very important. I want to know who *her* is in case *her* tries to act like an idiot. That way, I'll know the right ass to beat."

Chas chuckled because he knew that Jo was no match for Raven. But then again, he really didn't know Jo, so she might surprise him. *Damn,* he thought, *how in the hell did I get on Raven?* He didn't want to mention her name. To him, she was obsolete…a has been, a love of the past.

"Jo, who I've dated is not important, and besides, that is not what I wanted to discuss with you. I just wanted to share with you my diagnosis. The doctor thinks we caught it in time, though."

"Well, that's good news. I've known several men who had prostate cancer and lived to tell about it."

Chas shook his head. "What about those who didn't live to tell about it?" He walked to the window and stared out at nothing in particular.

She walked up behind him and placed her hand on his shoulder. "Chas, you have to be positive, sweetie. My girlfriend suffered with breast cancer and she fought her way through it. Now she's in remission and living her life. You have to be determined to beat this. You can't let it win."

Chas turned to her and smiled. "Thank you."

"For what?"

"For being so encouraging and lending your shoulder."

"That's what friends are for. Now, can we please get something to eat? I'm starving!"

"Sure," he chuckled, "but on one condition." She threw him a smirk. "You have to teach me to hand dance."

"Oh, is that it? Shucks, I can teach you to hand dance and some other things I won't get into at this time," she smiled, "but you will enjoy it better than the hand dancing!"

Chapter 36

Morgan slipped out of bed and tiptoed to the kitchen. Not wanting to wake Arthur, she slowly opened the sliding glass door and stepped out onto the deck. She inhaled the fresh morning air and smiled at the orange and yellow rays from the morning sunrise. She reclined in the lounge chair and contemplated preparing breakfast for Arthur. Then, she lowered her head and cried. She didn't want to kill her husband. She loved her husband, but he couldn't get away with cheating on her. She wondered if he told Raven about their chat in the hospital. Raven didn't act like she knew, but then again, it was hard to tell with Raven.

Morgan pulled herself to her feet, stretched, yawned, and headed for the kitchen. She reached in the refrigerator and grabbed the carton of eggs, milk, butter, link sausages, and pancake batter. She was about to prepare Arthur a meal he would never forget.

The rosebud vase stood in the middle of the wooden breakfast tray, surrounded by small plates of mixed fruits, scrambled eggs, sausages, pancakes topped with melting butter, and a tall glass of refreshing orange juice. A meal fit for a King.

Morgan tiptoed up the stairs and stood before the bedroom door. She took in several deep breaths, closed her eyes, and said a silent prayer. *"God forgive me, for I know what I'm about to do and I know it's not the right thing to do. But, I'm a woman scorned and he must pay. Please have mercy on me."*

She placed the tray on the floor, grabbed the doorknob, and gently turned until she heard the opening click. She slowly pushed the door open and heard Arthur's gentle snores. For a moment, she had second thoughts. However, it only lasted a moment. She bent down and picked up the tray, careful not to spill the juice or tumble over the rosebud vase.

"Rise and shine, sweetheart, time for breakfast," she sung, walking toward the bed. "Arthur, wake up. I've made you breakfast in bed and you're going to love it." A wicked grin peeked at the corners of her mouth.

Arthur swallowed hard before opening his eyes. "Good morning," he yawned. "Wow, what a treat," he said as he pulled himself up in the bed. He propped up the pillows behind him and folded his hands behind his head. "What do I owe the pleasure of this?"

"Well, I don't know," she said as she placed the tray strategically over his thighs. "I guess I'm making up for last night."

"About last night, Morgan. We really do need to talk about the Raven situation."

"There's nothing to talk about. You had an affair with my sister, and you said it was over." She leaned back and smiled, all the while crying inside. "Right?"

"Yes, and it is over, but we need to talk about it."

"We can talk later. Enjoy your breakfast for now." She leaned in and kissed him on the forehead. She smiled and glared into his eyes. "Eat up, baby."

She let him touch her hand. "I do love you, Morgan."

She grabbed him by the face, looked into his eyes, and lied, "I love you, too," before she backed away and left the room. Well, she didn't really lie to him, but she had to turn off her emotions since she had seasoned his eggs with a low dosage of rat poisoning.

Morgan sat patiently at the kitchen table, her hands crossed across her abdomen. Her thumbs intertwined as she envisioned Arthur choking on his eggs. A smile crept across her face. She tilted her head back and inhaled deeply, slowly exhaling. Her demeanor had changed. She was no longer the loving wife who'd do anything for her husband. Now, she was cold, calculating, and callous.

She looked at her watch. Fifteen minutes had passed. She braced herself and slowly proceeded to the foot of the staircase. She looked upward and called out, "Arthur." She stood quietly and heard nothing. She called out, "Arthur," again. No response. She gently placed the ball of her barefoot on the bottom step and proceeded up the stairs toward the bedroom. At the edge of the bedroom door, she peeked around the corner and saw Arthur.

"Hey, you," he said. His eyes displayed a glassy look and his skin looked cold and clammy.

Morgan swallowed hard. "How was breakfast?"

"It was good, but I think I'm coming down with something. I don't feel so hot."

She walked toward the bed. "No? Well, the flu *is* going around." She pressed the palm of her hand against his forehead. "You *are* feeling warm." She removed the tray from his lap and gently sat it on the floor. She took note of the missing eggs.

Arthur grabbed his stomach and leaned over. "My stomach is cramping."

She stood erect. "Maybe you need to use the bathroom," she suggested, smirking.

"Yeah, maybe you're right."

Arthur felt lightheaded and woozy as he pulled himself out of bed and waddled to the bathroom. Before closing the door behind him, he bent over and heaved.

Morgan sat on the bed and crossed her legs, listening as Arthur heaved his insides into the toilet. She propped her elbow on her knee and rested her chin in the palm of her hand. "Poor baby," she said, sighing heavily.

Chapter 37

Being ignored was an act she loathed, especially when the person ignoring her was the man she loved. Raven pressed her finger against the doorbell. She stood impatiently as no one answered. She knew he was there because his car was parked in the driveway. She pressed the doorbell once more. Then, after no answer, she knocked as hard as she could.

Raven tightened her lips and yelled to the top of her lungs. "Chas, I know you're in there! I see your car in the driveway!" She knew he was there and the silence was killing her. She reached in her purse for her cellular phone. She flipped it open, pressed voice command, and ordered the phone to, "Call Chas." The phone rang six times before going to voicemail. She stomped her foot and switched her weight from one foot to the other before stomping off to her car and peeling off down the street.

Chas stared at the ceiling as Jo's silky smooth leg clung to him while she played in his thick, curly chest hair. Her head fit perfectly in the hollow between his shoulder and neck.

"Why didn't you answer the door?"

Chas tightened his grip around her and gently rocked. "It wasn't important."

"Well, whoever it was, they thought it to be important. I thought she was going to knock the door down."

He stroked the curve of her hip. "Did it scare you?"

Her skin tingled from his touch. "No, not at all. I feel safe with you, Chas." Something in his manner relaxed her.

Softly his breath fanned her face. "Good, because I'd never let anything happen to you." He kissed her forehead and hugged her tighter. "I'm missing you," he whispered. His breath was hot against her ear.

She laughed softly. "I'm right here, silly."

With his finger, he traced a path from her hip, over her belly, and down toward her sex where he stopped at her opening. "This is what I'm missing."

Her heart fluttered at the thought of him entering her once more. "You're going to make me fall for you," she toyed.

She eased open her legs and made way for his finger to play beyond her opening. Her breaths were soft and quick as his finger wiggled inside her. He covered her lips with his as he pulled her on top of him, opening his legs as she mounted him. She had no intentions of backing away from what he desired. Her head tilted back with enjoyment as her firm, plump breast stood to attention, jutting forward and begging for his embrace. He palmed her breasts and gently squeezed them. He watched her nipples swell in size, and then he closed his eyes and tweaked her nipples between his fingers. She cooed and leaned forward, kissing him softly on the lips. He grabbed the back of her head and tossed her onto her back.

Chas knelt over her, straddled her, and then opened her mouth with his fingers. He slid his hardness into her mouth with a quick downward motion. She closed her eyes and drew on it, smelling the delicious fragrance of his pubic hair and tasting the saltiness of his skin, his penis nudging the back of her throat again and again. She moaned in time with his movements, and when suddenly he drew himself out, she gasped.

He laid down on her, parted her legs, and drove into her passionately. She felt herself explode with pleasure. Her back arched so rigidly that she lifted his weight with her. She thrust her hips in almost a snapping motion, and when he came at last, he collapsed.

"How was it?" he asked.

"You're kidding me, right?"

Chas rolled off of her and onto his back. "You didn't like it?"

Jo laughed and shook her head in disbelief. "Baby, it was the best love I've ever had. You are so passionate and sensual. It was so intense. I felt like our spirits bonded."

"I tried to get all up in you. I wanted to feel every inch of you, Jo."

"Yes, I know, and you were all up in there, too."

Chas reached over and caressed her face. "This feels so right. You know?"

Jo pulled herself up and leaned back against the headboard. "Yeah," she smiled, "I know." She pulled the covers over her thighs and patted the spot where she wanted him to lay his head. "Let's talk for a bit."

Before lowering his head to her lap, Chas softly pecked Jo on her breast. "What's on your mind?" he asked.

"You're on my mind."

"I'm listening."

"Have you decided about your treatments?"

"No, haven't really thought much else about it."

"I don't want you to put this off, baby."

"Oh, I'm not going to do that, sweetie. I have a meeting with Dr. McKnight in a few days. We'll decide then the best treatment for me."

"Good," she said, followed by a heavy sigh.

"You want to know who was at the door, don't you?"

"Don't be silly. That's your business, and I'm sure you'll take care of it."

Chas raised his head and gazed into her eyes. "You're lying," he chuckled.

Jo playfully smacked him upside the head. "Maybe so, but I'm not going there. Besides, you are your own man. I have no control over who you see."

He pulled back the covers. "I'm only seeing you," he whispered, burying his face between her thighs. "I love the way you smell," he said.

Jo fell out with laughter. "Boy, you are crazy!" She leaned her head back against the wall and said, "I need to get ready to get out of here."

Chas grabbed hold of her hips. "Why are you rushing?"

"Well, I'm not rushing. It's not like I have somewhere to go, but I thought you would want your space."

"I'm enjoying the space I'm in, with you."

Chapter 38

The bathroom door slowly opened. Arthur stood in the doorway; his shoulders slouched over in agony.

"How are you feeling?" Morgan asked, examining her fresh manicure.

"Not so hot. I need to lie down for a bit."

Morgan rose to her feet and started to tidy up the bed. "It must be the stomach flu." She fluffed the pillows.

Arthur sat down on the bed and looked up at her. "This doesn't feel like the stomach flu." His eyes were glossy and bulging from his head. The whites of his eyes had turned red.

"Well, I'm sure that's all it is," she said, grabbing him by the feet and raising his legs into the bed. "Get some rest," she sighed, pulling the cover over him. "What else can I get you, honey?"

He eyed her suspiciously. "There was blood and dark yellow mucus in my vomit, Morgan."

"And?"

"And it doesn't come from having a stomach virus," he snapped. "Do you hate me that much, Morgan, you would try and poison me?"

"Arthur, I don't appreciate your accusations!" she snapped back. "I hope you feel better real soon!" She stormed out of the bedroom, slamming the door behind her.

Arthur studied the half-eaten breakfast long and hard. He removed the pillow from the pillowcase and reached for the plate. He placed the plate into the pillowcase and tucked it under the bed, then leaned back and glared at the closed door.

"Would she really try to kill me?" he mumbled.

Chapter 39

In a boring huff, Raven plopped down before her computer and signed on to AOL, something she hadn't done in quite some time. Her past experiences with the Internet left a lot to be desired, especially her encounter with Michael Anthony — a true piece of work.

She was puzzled about Chas. He wouldn't return her calls. He wouldn't answer the door. What was going on with him? She couldn't imagine him having anyone else in his life. He was madly in love with her and didn't have eyes for anyone. Or so she thought.

"Fuck 'em," she mumbled. She kicked off her shoes and headed for the bedroom. "I really don't need his ass no way."

Raven stood on the tips of her toes and shuffled through the top of her closet. "What the hell did I do with it?" she asked herself as she felt around for the little box. A smile parted her lips when her fingers touched the small cardboard box. She tore open the box, tossed it on the floor, and made a beeline for her bed.

Her jeans and panties fell down around her feet. She didn't bother stepping out of them before she fell back on the bed, raised her legs in the air, and placed the silver bullet between her pouting vaginal lips. Her mouth fell open as she increased the speed using the hand control. Her hips pushed forward and side-to-side, like she was having fits. Her face distorted and her legs shot straight out before her. Her head felt like Mount Saint Helen's; ready to explode at any minute. Her body shook and shivered as she peaked at full climax.

Raven dropped her legs to the floor, tossed the silver bullet to the side, and panted, "To hell with Chas. I have my bullet."

Chapter 40

Arthur leaned in the doorway and looked around the office. "Stan, got those results for me?"

"Sure do." Stan smiled at Arthur. "How goes it?"

Arthur sashayed into the office and pulled up a chair. "I can't complain. I assume life's treating you well?"

Stan sat at his desk and pulled himself forward. "Things couldn't be better. As you requested, I ran the test myself." He reached inside the desk drawer and pulled out an eight by ten envelope, handing it to Arthur. "You were right on the money with your assumption."

As their eyes met, Arthur felt a shock run through him. "Rat poisoning, huh?"

"Yep, and the recipient of the tasty treat got off lucky. There wasn't enough of a dosage to kill, only to make one sick as a dog."

Arthur was momentarily speechless. He managed to shake his head in agreement, but at the same time he was torn up inside. He knew Morgan was capable of many things, but never attempted murder. That was Raven's specialty.

Arthur stood up and extended his hand. "Hey, man, thanks a lot. I appreciate it. Anything I can do for you let me know."

"It's all good. I'm glad I could do it." Stan hesitated and stroked his chin in deep thought. "Think we need to bring the police into this?"

"No, I don't think so. One of my patients…a disgruntled wife." Arthur faked a chuckle.

"Women," Stan blurted. "You know what they say?"

Arthur smiled and nodded his head. "Yeah, man, you can't live with them and you can't live without them."

"Right, except I can live without a bitch trying to put me in an early grave."

Arthur forced a smile. "I hear ya, man. Take it easy."

"Yeah, you do the same."

Arthur nodded his head, smiled, and entered the busy hallway of the Washington Hospital Center. He closed the door behind him and took several steps before coming to a stop. He leaned against the wall and tilted his head back, tapping it against the wall. Hot, gritty tears welled in his eyes, burning like hot sand. He closed his eyes and cried softly. He slid down to the floor and cradled himself.

"Are you alright, Sir?" a passerby asked.

Arthur nodded his head and wiped his eyes. He gathered himself, using the back of his hand to wipe his nose. He pulled himself to his feet and stood in a daze. Deep down in the core of his soul, he knew he deserved a much more lethal dose than what Morgan administered. Sure, he and Morgan had been through their trials and tribulations, but she did not deserve any of this. He betrayed her and was determined to make it right. He was going home to his wife. It was time to come clean. Besides, he valued his life.

Chapter 41

Morgan kissed Franklin on the forehead and laid him face down in the crib. She covered him with a soft, blue blanket and stroked the back of his soft, delicate head.

"Sleep tight, my prince," she whispered. "Mama's little man." She tightened the belt around her robe and looked around the nursery.

It was the perfect baby's nursery. Fit for a baby who would have everything his heart desired. The soft, baby blue-painted walls were the backdrops for Tweety Bird and Sylvester. In the far corner sat a light blue rocking horse, with a square recessed seat in the horse's back, a detailed molded horse's face and head on the front, a molded tail on the back, and curved rockers on the base. Morgan loved that horse and purchased it more so for her, than for Franklin. Not too far from the rocking horse was the gift from Raven, a white square baby stroller that rolled on four blue wheels and had a blue push handle, with a blue canopy that had scalloped edges and a huge blue bow attached. She especially adored the white dresser/changing table because it was a gift from the staff from Arthur's practice. The walk-in closet was filled with clothing ranging in size from six months to 3T, thanks to Raven.

Morgan kissed her fingers and gently pressed them against Franklin's cheek. She smiled and said, "I love you, Frankie," then turned on the baby monitor and settled into her bed for a badly needed nap. She made it a point to sleep when Franklin slept. And since Arthur wasn't home, she would only have one baby to worry about.

Morgan relaxed in a fetal position, pulled the covers snuggly up around her chin, and closed her eyes. Within minutes, she was softly purring.

It all looked too familiar. *What in the world,* Morgan thought. The burnt orange carpeting and green velvet sofa covered in plastic. The old breakfront filled to the hinges with mismatched china. Pierre, the black toy poodle, darted around barking non-stop and Chanel No. 5 wafted in the air.

Mama darted by Morgan in a huff, almost knocking her down. "Franklin, we're going to be late," she snapped.

"I'm coming, woman. Don't rush me. You're the one who took an hour in the bathroom," Daddy fussed, charging on her heels.

Morgan reached out toward him as he rushed by, swiping at his shoulder. Her hand went through him, as if he wasn't really there, kind of ghostlike. *What in the hell is going on,* she thought. Out of habit, she tugged at the belt of her robe and tightened it around her waist.

"Daddy?" she called out, but Franklin didn't respond.

Two girls darted down the stairs and to the front door. Morgan couldn't believe her eyes. She blinked her eyes several times, trying to make sense of all that was happening. *It can't be,* she thought.

Thirteen-year-old Morgan stood in the front door, frantically waving. "Bye, Mama. Bye, Daddy. Bring us something back," she yelled

"We will, sweetheart. Take care of your sister. We'll be back soon."

"Okay, Mama! But you know Raven don't listen to me."

Mama looked at Raven. "Raven Nicole Ward, you do what your sister tells you to do. You hear me?"

"What if she tells me to jump off the roof, Mama?"

Mama smirked, but wasn't amused. "Yes! If she tells you to jump, you had better ask how high!"

"Come on, Margaret, get in the car," Daddy cried. "We never get anywhere on time."

"Oh, alright, Franklin!" Mama blew her girls a kiss and hopped in the car. "Love you both."

"For goodness sakes, Margaret, you act like we're going to be gone for a month. We'll be back in a few hours."

"I know, but they've never stayed home alone, Franklin."

"They'll be fine."

As Mama and Daddy pulled away from the curb, Morgan palmed Raven in the face, pushing her inside the house.

"You heard what Mama said. You have to do what I tell you to do or else I'm gon' beat your ass like Mama did earlier," Morgan laughed. "By the way, is your butt still sore?"

"Shut up, and I'm gonna tell you're cussin'!"

"Mama always said a hard head made for a soft behind. I guess your head ain't so hard no more."

"Shut up and leave me alone!" Raven stormed upstairs. "I'm going outside," she declared.

Morgan darted to the foot of the staircase. "No, you're not. You know we can't go out when Mama and Daddy ain't here."

"I don't care and they ain't coming back no way."

"What do you mean, they ain't coming back?"

"You heard me!" Raven yelled and then slammed her bedroom door.

Morgan found herself straddling the double mustard yellow line as she stood in the middle of Fort DuPont Park, surrounded by trees and the pending sunset. The red 1970 Chevy Nova swiftly swerved toward her at a high rate of speed. She tried to move, but her feet felt like lead sinking into hot tar.

"Oh my God!" she hysterically cried, frantically trying to move her feet. Panic like she'd never known before welled in her throat. "Somebody please help me!" she cried.

The car continued toward her. It was close enough where she could make out the occupants. Her eyes widened and her pulse raced. "Mama! Daddy! No, God, no!"

Her mother's face was distorted with fear and her father was desperately trying to regain control of the car. Her mother's screams were horrifying and spine tingling, filling the deserted park, as the Nova connected with the tall pine tree.

Morgan yelled to the top of her lungs and began to hyperventilate. Smoke exuded from the folded hood of the car. Her father's head rested against the steering wheel, as the gash down the side of his face gushed with red and protruding flesh. Her mother had ejected through the windshield, her flesh stripped from her torso.

Morgan sprung up in the bed. Pools of perspiration trickled down her face. She felt lightheaded and a knot formed in her stomach, getting tighter with each breath. She looked around the room, confused. She felt pain and heartache. What Morgan had locked away in the attic of her memory had escaped. She felt cold and started to tremble.

"Oh, Mama and Daddy, I'm so sorry! I'm so sorry!" she cried loudly, her vision blinded by the salty tears. "I didn't know what to do. I was only a little girl. Oh, God, please forgive me. Please!"

Arthur's voice startled her. "Honey!" he called out from the foyer. He dropped his coat on the floor, slammed the front door, and darted up the stairs. "Baby, what's wrong? I heard you yelling, from outside. What's going on?" He stopped in his tracks. "Morgan, what in the world…"

She interrupted him before he could finish his thought. "I remember," she cried. "I had forgotten about it, didn't want to face it. But now I remember." She was shaking profusely.

Arthur dashed to her side and pulled her into him. "Try to calm down and tell me what you're talking about."

Morgan took slow deep breaths and closed her eyes. "I made myself forget about it because I didn't want to face reality."

Arthur swept the wet strands of hair from her forehead to the side of her head. She began to rock, back and forth. He kissed her on the forehead and embraced her tighter, trying to calm her.

"Can I get you anything?" he asked.

"No," she whispered. She stopped rocking and pulled away from his embrace, staring at him as if looking at a stranger. "I didn't want to kill you. I only wanted to make you feel the hurt I was feeling," she declared.

Arthur lowered his head and closed his eyes. Then, he raised his head and tilted it back as he opened his eyes and glared at the ceiling. "I deserved it."

"Yes, you did," she snapped.

"Morgan, I don't know what you want me to do. I mean, I knew it was wrong, but she had me by the fucking balls."

"I know," she said in a hushed tone. Her demeanor was now calm. "I know," she repeated.

Arthur looked at her in bewilderment. "I don't understand. I thought…"

She raised her hand to silence him. "I need to share something with you. Something I've never uttered to another living soul. It was a secret kept between me and Raven. When I was thirteen, my parents…" she hesitated. Arthur studied her intently, hanging on her every word. "They died in a car accident."

Arthur knew this already and desperately wanted her to get to the point. He'd never seen her so out of sorts before. It was really scaring him. She looked like she was about to lose it.

Morgan looked Arthur in the eyes with a cold stare. "It's my fault they're dead."

"That's crazy, Morgan. How can it be your fault?"

"No, it's my fault because I knew what she did."

"What are you talking about?" He leaned in closer. His gut feeling was gnawing at him, telling him Raven was involved – someway, somehow.

"Earlier that day, Raven had gotten into trouble. Mama whipped her, and good, too. I can't remember her getting a whipping worse than that one."

"I'm sure she deserved it." Arthur's tone was sarcastic and spiteful.

Morgan ignored his sarcasm and continued. "After our parents left, Raven announced she was going outside, knowing we weren't supposed to leave the house when Mama and Daddy weren't home. When I told her she wasn't going anywhere, she said it didn't matter what Mama and Daddy thought because they weren't coming back home." Morgan clutched tight to Arthur's hand and bawled hysterically.

"Are you trying to tell me that Raven had something to do with the accident?"

Morgan nodded her head profusely. "That's exactly what I'm saying."

"But how. . ."

"She was mad at Mama for giving her the beating of her life. There was a beehive attached to the side of the house. She knocked it down and swept it into a plastic bag. Then she placed it in the back seat of the car. The bees got out and attacked them while they were driving through DuPont Park, causing them to crash into a tree. My parents died instantly." Morgan wiped her dripping nose with the back of her hand. "I didn't tell anyone about it."

"Well, you were only thirteen. What did you know?"

"I knew that Raven killed my parents!" she yelled to the top of her lungs. She lunged into Arthur's arms and cried. "She took away two of the most important people in my life, and now you."

Tears streamed down Arthur's cheeks. He cradled her gently and rocked back and forth, calming her. "It's going to be alright, baby," he consoled.

Morgan broke their embrace. "She has to pay for all that she's done." A psychotic smile crept on her lips. "She took Mama and Daddy, but she's not going to have you, too."

"What do you have in mind?" he asked.

Morgan grabbed Arthur's sleeve and wiped her face, then smiled and leaned back against the headboard. "I don't know, but the evil has to stop before someone else gets hurt."

Arthur lowered his head. "It's too late."

Chapter 42

"Hey, you."

"Hey, back at you."

"How are you doing?"

"I'm doing good, and yourself?"

"Well, I'm a little anxious to know how your meeting went with your doctor."

Chas smiled at Jo's concern. "It went well. I'm going to do a few chemo treatments and all should be fine."

"Yeah? What do you think about getting a second opinion?"

"I'm pretty comfortable with Dr. McKnight. Besides, he's been through it, so that helps a lot in knowing that."

"Oh, I see. Well, I only want the best for you, Chas. I'm here for you. Whatever you need me to do, consider it done."

"I know and thanks," he hesitated, becoming sentimental and teary-eyed. "Hey listen, you have plans this evening?"

"What do you have in mind?"

"Dare you ask such a loaded question?" he teased.

"Oh my…on second thought, surprise me," she chuckled.

"Be careful what you ask for. I'm very good at surprising people."

"Bring it on," she responded in a reassuring tone.

"Not a problem. See you here at eight."

"Until then…muah!"

Chas looked at the receiver and smiled before returning it to its base. He shook his head and smiled. "She's in for a treat, and has no clue," he chuckled to himself.

Chapter 43

The knot in Arthur's stomach tightened as he listened intently to Morgan.

"She's evil," Morgan said, twisting the ends of the pillowcase between her thumb and index fingers. "She's the evil twin of Damien." Morgan rocked back and forth, a deranged smile creeping across her face. "Rosemary's baby is more like it," she chuckled.

Arthur chuckled, too. "Raven *is* a piece of work."

Morgan faced him, her deranged smile quickly turning to a look of sadness. "How did she get her hands on you?"

Arthur mentally waved the white flag. It was time for him to come clean. He could feel the humiliation moving from the pit of his bowels up to his throat. He didn't want to hurt Morgan, but the truth had to be told. He loved her more than anything and knew that telling the truth would free him from the private dungeon he'd been living in for months. It was stifling and he was ready to break free.

Morgan swung her legs to the edge of the bed and braced her feet against the floor. She leaned in closer to Arthur, closed her eyes, and inhaled deeply. She loved the way her man smelled. On a whim, she gave him Velocity by Mary Kay for his birthday and he loved it — practically bathing in it. She took his hands in hers and caressed them gently. His hands were soft as a baby's bottom.

She loved the way Arthur took care of himself. She could see why Raven would be interested in him. Even a blind woman could see how good of a man he was.

Arthur's eyes traveled over her face, to her protruding cleavage, and then rested on her long fingers. She was an angel. He wrapped his fingers around her delicate wrists. He longed to love her, kiss her delicate face and her curved lips.

"Morgan, I…" She pressed her index finger against his soft, full lips while shaking her head to silence him.

"I have a confession to make, as well," she said. "I wanted you to feel what I was feeling. The pain of being betrayed by a man I've loved all of my life and a sister…well, there's no excuse for her. Sisters keep their hands to themselves. There's a fine line you don't cross, and she crossed it big time!" The lines in her forehead were more evident, describing exactly how she was feeling. "I'm more hurt behind her actions than I am yours."

Arthur lowered his head.

"Uh huh, don't do that, honey. Don't lower your head in embarrassment. You weren't feeling that way when you were fucking my sister."

A tear dropped from his eye and onto her foot.

"Look at me, Arthur."

He slowly raised his head. His eyes glistened with a red overcast.

"You and me…we've been through some hard times in our marriage." Arthur nodded his head in agreement. "And we'll get through this episode, as well."

An ounce of hope shined brightly on his face. "You're not going to leave me?"

"No, I'm not going to leave you. Franklin needs his father and I…well, I don't quite know what I need. But, I'm thinking of my son right now."

Arthur dropped his head into her lap. "Morgan, I am so sorry." He wept between her thighs. "Why didn't you kill me?"

Morgan's mouth fell open as she stared off into the distance. "How did you know?"

Arthur spoke into her lap. "I know the side effects of ingesting poison. I'm a doctor." Arthur raised his head to come face to face with her breast. He leaned in and gently kissed them. She sighed. Arthur knelt down before her and untied the belt attached to her robe. "I love you so much, baby."

Morgan nodded and caressed his head. "I love you, too." Her cry was internal, but her tears were evident as he cupped her full breasts in the palms of his hands.

Arthur took her hardened nipple into his mouth and gently sucked. Her breasts were still filled with Franklin's milk. Arthur tasted her as he squeezed very gently, aware of the tenderness of her breast.

Morgan parted her legs, welcoming him to a place she'd longed for him to be. "Make love to me," she whispered in his ear. "Make love to your wife."

Arthur kissed her on the lips, the chin, around her neck, down her chest and stopped at her abdomen. With his hands, he spread her legs open a little more and admired her beauty. "You're a very beautiful woman, Morgan. I was a fool to think…"

"Not now," she whispered. She lay down on the bed and raised her legs, resting the balls of her feet on the edge of the bed. He kissed each toe before leaving a trail from her knee to the center of her love.

Morgan's body quivered with pleasure. She wanted him more now than she ever wanted him before. She parted her legs wider, feeling the spread of her pubic lips. Arthur nuzzled his nose in her pubic hairs and stroked his tongue against her clitoris.

"Oooh," Morgan moaned. She closed her eyes tight and gently bit down on her bottom lip. Arthur covered her clitoris with his mouth as his tongue played beneath the hood. "Ohhhhhhhhhh…" Morgan pushed her hips into his face, feeling the bridge of his nose stroking the top of her sex. He inserted his finger and stroked the top of her vagina, concentrating on the swelling knot. Morgan felt like she was about to explode. Her body trembled. Her legs felt weak. She wrapped them around his neck. Morgan's breath became uneven, and she felt the moisture rushing through her vaginal canal rest around her pubic lips.

Arthur unwrapped her legs from around his neck and raised them in the air, gently bending them back toward her. Her buttocks rose in the air, and his tongue gently stroked her exposed anus.

Morgan moaned. The pleasure he was giving her was different. Intense. It was wonderful and, at the same time, unbelievable.

Arthur returned his attention to her clitoris, sucking profusely and bringing her to a full climax. Her body jittered and her breast jutted upward. Her erect nipples pointed toward the ceiling as she toyed with them between her fingers, enhancing her pleasure.

Morgan lowered her legs, allowing them to dangle at the side of the bed. "Wow," was all she could muster. Then, she asked, "Is that what you do to her?"

Arthur fell backward onto the floor in defeat. He pulled his knees to his chest and stared at the floor in deep thought before he responded. "When I make love to you, I'm doing just that...loving you inside and out. When I was with her, it was only sex because that's all she wanted. She wanted what you had, Morgan. Don't you get that yet? She wanted the husband, a baby, and a beautiful home. She wanted your life, and she was prepared to get it anyway she could."

Morgan covered her eyes with her hands and sobbed. "I can't imagine..."

"Morgan, my love for you is strong, and she could see that. She wanted to be loved that way, too."

"But she has Chas, and he loves her just as much."

"True, but it isn't the same to Raven. It has to be identical or nothing at all."

Morgan crawled beneath the covers, propping her elbow on the pillow and resting her head in her hand.

"Baby, your sister doesn't admire you. She envies you."

Morgan stared off deep in thought before responding. "Right after our car accident, I think I died." Arthur gave her a funny look, but decided not to interrupt. "I saw Mama and Daddy. They told me I had to go back because you needed me here, and so did Franklin. I didn't want to come back, Arthur. I've missed Mama and Daddy so much. I wanted to stay with them. But, it wasn't my time and I turned to come back. Daddy's last words to me were, 'Keep an eye on that sister of yours. She's a rotten seed.' Daddy knew what was going on and he was warning me."

"That's deep, honey."

"Yeah, it is…"

"Morgan, I met a woman." Morgan's eyes widened and her lips parted. "Hear me out. I am a weak man. The woman had come on so strong, I didn't know what to do or think. I knew, deep in my heart, I didn't want her, but there was something about her that aroused my curiosity. So, I took her to dinner. During that dinner, it was discovered that she was Ramone's wife."

Morgan gasped. "What?" She sprang upright in the bed. "I didn't know Ramone was married!"

"Neither did Raven until I asked for her help."

"Her help to do what?"

"Well, during dinner, I told Reneè I couldn't see her again. That I was happily married and it was wrong for me to have invited her to dinner in the first place."

"You got that shit right," Morgan snapped.

Arthur continued. "Reneè wasn't taking no for an answer. She called the office and got my pager number. When she paged me, of course I called back. That's how she got my cell phone number. After that, she rung my cell phone off the hook, threatening to come to the home and do harm to you."

"I wish she would've tried! I would've whipped her ass!"

Arthur smiled and continued. "So, I enlisted Raven to help me out. When I told her who was *stalking* me, she was more than happy to assist me."

In a sarcastic tone, Morgan blurted out, "I bet she was!"

"Now they are dead."

Morgan couldn't believe her ears...or could she? "Oh my God," she whispered. "Arthur, what are you saying?"

"I'm saying that Raven blew both their brains out all because of me. She's a murderer and I'm the accomplice."

Chapter 44

Raven stood in the mirror and caressed her breast. She smiled at the perkiness of each breast and their perfect round areolas. She was tempted to stroke her nipple with her tongue, but her tongue wasn't long enough. She released her breast and allowed her fingertips to travel down to the opening of her lips, where she squeezed and teased, tugging at the pubic area. She tossed her head back and fingered her clitoris gently. Just then, the ringing of the telephone interrupted her silent moans and private pleasing session.

"Hello," she answered, annoyed at being interrupted.

"Raven?"

"Who wants to know?"

"Hi, this is Cassie."

"Who?"

"Cassie. You and I met at Tradewinds. Remember? I was Marcy's friend."

Raven bit her lip to stifle a grin. "How did you get my number?"

"I called information and you weren't listed."

"Yes, I know. This is why I can't understand how you got my number."

"Please don't be upset. It was important that I speak with you, so I phoned a friend who works for Verizon. Against her better judgment, she gave me your number."

"Humph, remind me to call her boss in the morning." Raven slipped into her silk leopard print robe and released a sigh of irritation. "Well, what can I do for you?"

"I'd like to meet with you…"

Defensively, Raven replied, "I'm no carpet muncher. I only taste my own pussy."

"That is not what I meant," she said calmly, realizing the ignorance she was up against. "I would like to talk about Cassie."

"What about her?"

"I didn't know any of her friends and…"

"We weren't friends," Raven snapped.

Cassie remained calm, even though Raven was as nasty and snappish as she could get. "I understand. I'm sorry I bothered you."

"Sure," she said, clicking the off button and tossing the phone on the bed. "I'm horny," she announced as she walked to the bathroom, scratching her behind.

Raven drew a warm bubble bath, dropped her robe to the floor, and emerged herself beneath the bubbles. Feeling relaxed and worry-free, she closed her eyes and dozed off.

It seemed like she had been sleeping for hours, but the water was still warm and relaxing. She blinked her eyes several times, trying to make out the figure sitting on the commode. She slightly rose up, not believing her eyes.

"You're still soaking in the tub, I see."

"I-I-I don't believe it," Raven stuttered. "Is that really you?"

"Well, it's not a bag of nachos."

"Oh Mama…"

"Raven, I don't know what you've done, but you better find a way to clean up this mess you've gotten yourself into."

"Oh Mama, what are you talking about? I'm doing great."

"No, you're not. You're sleeping with your sister's husband, for God's sake!"

"No, I'm…"

Mama raised her hand to silence her. "I don't want to hear any of your lies. Your father and I are so disappointed, but we aren't surprised. After all, look at what you did to us."

Raven sat in silence. Although she and Morgan had vowed to never bring it up again, she never forgot the despicable act she performed against her mother, causing her parents' untimely death.

"You were a devil child then and you're worse now. You listen to me, and you listen to me real good, Raven. If you don't straighten up and fly right, you will surely meet your match."

"Mama, I don't know what you're talking about."

"You just keep on acting like you don't have a clue. I'm telling you, child, you're about to meet your match."

Raven laid back and turned her head. The look in her mother's eyes was one of complete hatred. She closed her eyes and cried herself to sleep.

She awoke from what felt like a bad dream. She looked around the bathroom and her mother was nowhere to be found.

"It was only a dream," she sighed.

The bath water was below room temperature, and it felt like she was sitting in a swimming pool. Hopping up from the tub, she reached for a towel and wrapped it around her. Small puddles followed to her bedroom. She reached for the phone and called Morgan, needing to talk to her about her dream. She wanted to know what it all meant. Truth be told, the dream freaked her out and she was scared as hell. To her dismay, there was no answer at Morgan's, so she left a message.

She sat on the edge of the bed, trying to figure out what Mama was talking about. After all, she hadn't done anything to anyone who didn't deserve it. Besides, she wasn't going to let people walk over her or betray her. It wasn't right, and she wasn't going to let anyone get away with it. In regards to Arthur, she believed she wasn't doing anything wrong there, either. He wanted her just as much as she wanted him. It's called matters of the heart. She loved Arthur and she knew he loved her, too. He was only biding his time with Morgan. If it wasn't for Franklin, he would've left Morgan months ago. As far as Raven was concerned, Morgan didn't know what she had, and if she wasn't going to do right by her man, then Raven was planning to pick up her slack. Anyway, better her sister fuck her husband than some stranger, like Reneè.

Her attention turned to Cassie. Maybe she had been a little hard on her. However, she wasn't interested in Marcy or what Cassie had to say. She needed Marcy for one reason and one reason only, to get back at Jay. But then again, if memory served her right, Cassie was the reason why Marcy and Jay broke up in the first place, which only meant that Cassie was dealing with Jay while he was with Raven.

Raven immediately jumped into payback mode. After reaching in the nightstand drawer and retrieving an ink pen, she reached for the phone and checked the caller ID. She jotted down Cassie's number and hit redial.

"Hi Cassie, this is Raven."

"Oh, hello."

"Listen, sorry about the way I treated you. I must be PMSing or something. I would love to get together. When do you have in mind?"

"I completely understand. How about Friday? We can do drinks somewhere."

"Sure, Friday sounds good. Where do you live?"

"In Oxon Hill."

"How about Martini's or Club Elite?"

"I'm closer to Martini's."

"Martini's it is. Eight o'clock?"

"See you then. Bye, Raven."

"See ya." Raven hung up the phone. "Wouldn't wanna be ya," she chuckled.

Chapter 45

Chas had set the mood with dancing flames from scented candles, Teddy Pendergrass crooning in the background, and a bottle of Riesling wine chilling in a glass bucket.

"You've really outdone yourself this time," Jo teased.

"You think? It's nothing."

"Oh, you have dinner like this everyday?"

They both laughed. "No, only on special occasions."

She gently hiked up her dress and crossed her legs, exposing the thickest part of her thigh. "What's the occasion?"

Chas sat down beside her and extended a glass of wine. "Well, let's just say that I'm celebrating the good news."

Jo tilted her head to the side. "Are you going to tell me this good news?"

"Let's make a toast first."

Jo raised her glass. "To a wonderful friendship."

"And here's to a beautiful woman. You have made me very happy in the short time I've known you."

They tapped their glasses together, took a sip, and then kissed.

"So, the news, Chas."

"Oh yeah, almost forgot. I had my appointment with Dr. McKnight today, and it seems as if the lab had mixed up my test results."

Jo leaned forward. "What are you saying, Chas?"

"I'm saying that I have a lifetime to persuade you to see me exclusively."

Tears welled in Jo's eyes. "No cancer?"

"Not an ounce."

"Thank you, Jesus!"

"Amen to that!" Chas leaned back against the sofa. "You know, life has a way of making you see things clearly. I've realized that tomorrow is not promised to anyone."

"You're just realizing that?" she chuckled. "I learned that a long time ago when it seemed as if everyone around me was dying like flies."

He turned toward her. "Jo, I haven't lived my life selfishly. I've always been the one to give than to receive. I stay out of trouble and don't dibble dabble in drama. I guess I'm saying all of this to say that I need someone…no, I want someone in my life. Someone I can trust and never have to worry about betraying me. You know what I mean?"

"Yes, I know. I'm lonely, too."

"No, I'm not lonely. I love being with me. I miss all that comes with an honest, trusting, and loving relationship. Jo, you ignite a fire inside of me. You know, that kind of fire where I get gratification just talking to you or looking at you. I don't always have to have my hands on you. Our conversations are on a higher level than I'm used to. You are an intelligent, sexy woman. You can talk about any and everything under the sun. You're full of class…and I love you."

Jo sat for a moment in silence. "For once, I'm speechless."

"Don't say a word. Let me just admire your beauty."

"How about you admire my beauty from up there," she said, nodding her head toward the stairs and up to the bedroom.

"I was trying to be good."

Jo stood up and began unbuttoning her dress. "And I'm trying to be naughty tonight," she said as her dress billowed down around her feet.

Chas gasped in excitement. He felt himself rising and the urge to grab her. Her matching black lace panty ensemble turned him on even more. He loved to see a woman who cared about her undergarments.

Jo extended her hand and escorted Chas to his bedroom. The fire was already a great blaze from when Chas built it prior to her arrival. The curtains were drawn and the bed had been turned back. Jo quivered with excitement as she crawled on the bed and tooted her behind in the air.

"Spank me," she ordered. Chas didn't utter a sound, but obliged her instead. The first smack was soft and gentle. "Harder," she instructed. The second smack was slightly harder, and Jo moaned slightly. Again, she instructed, "Harder." Chas raised his arm in the air and swung down across her buttocks. Jo gave a soft cry. "Again until I tell you to stop." Chas obliged her again, again, and again, until her buttocks had turned blush red and whelps had begun to form.

Jo turned over on her back and raised her legs as Chas removed his erect penis from his britches and mounted her. He leaned down and kissed her lips while teasing her pubic lips, before thrusting himself inside her orifice.

She cried out. She wrapped her arms around his neck and felt his penis bathed with her juices. "Fuck me harder," she whispered in his ear. "Please, baby, I want to feel you inside me. Harder, please," she softly cried. Chas forced it in deeper, rubbing against some mysterious core in her, sending the ecstasy washing through her so she was giving great guttural moans. His thrusts came faster and faster and then he, too, gave a soft cry, holding her close to him with her breasts pressed firmly against his chest.

"I love you, too," she confessed.

Chapter 46

As much as she loved music and dancing, the club scene wasn't Cassie's cup of tea. So, she was excited when Raven phoned to suggest they meet for coffee instead.

Cassie's deep, rich mocha skin was smooth and unblemished. Not a wrinkle in sight. Her long curly locks were pinned on top of her head. Tendrils fell down around her brow, as if she had just finished making love. At the ripe age of fifty, she was more fit and voluptuous than the average thirty year old.

Cassie stood at the counter and sipped a cup of piping hot chocolate latté. The current issue of *The Afro American Newspaper* was tucked firmly under her arm. She paid for her latté and sought out an empty table in the busiest coffee shop in town, Starbucks. She placed her purse on the table and gracefully sat in the chair, crossing her long, curvaceous legs. Lightly, she fingered a loose tendril of hair from her face and began perusing her newspaper. After a minute of reading, she folded the paper, laid it on the table, sipped her latté, and eyed the place. Her eyes stopped abruptly on the petite figure with perky supple breast and curved hips. Her face was soft and her lips were full and daintily painted a pale glossy pink.

Raven looked in her direction, when their eyes met. Raven's smile was warm and inviting, making her feel warm and fuzzy, stirring a slight twinge between her thighs.

Cassie quickly looked away and focused her attention on the newspaper before her.

"Hey girl," Raven greeted.

Cassie looked up at Raven and stammered over her thoughts, trying to find something to say that didn't make her sound like the complete idiot she was feeling like.

"Usually, when someone says hello to you, the courteous response is hello."

"Hey girl, I'm sorry. You caught me off guard," Cassie responded, smiling sheepishly.

"Sorry I'm late. Been here long?"

"Uh, no, a few minutes."

Raven returned the smile and took a seat. "Anything worth reading?" she asked, nodding toward the newspaper.

"Same shit, different day."

Cassie admired Raven's beauty. She could see why Marcy would've been so enamored by her. To Cassie, Raven seemed gentle, serenely wise and beautiful. What a handsome package, and one that was turning Cassie completely on.

"Cassie, do you mind if I ask you a question?" Cassie nodded and continued to sip her latté. "What is it that you see in other women?" Cassie swallowed hard and rested her forehead in the palm of her hand. "Oh, I'm sorry. I didn't mean to offend."

"I'm not offended, just tired of the same old question being asked, day in and day out."

"You don't have to answer it, Cassie. It's okay."

"No, I don't mind. The same thing you look for in a man, I look for in a woman."

Raven burst into laughter. "A stiff dick?"

Cassie shot her an annoyed look. "If you can find a woman with a stiff dick, become her agent because you'll surely be rich." She was sick of being asked the same question, as if being with a woman didn't require the same love and compassion as with a man.

"Sorry, I didn't mean to offend you."

"I've been with men and women. Trust me, I'd much rather be with a woman."

Raven thought back to her escapade with Marcy and decided to hold her tongue. "So, you said you wanted to talk about Marcy. I don't know if I can tell you much. I really didn't know her that well."

"I'd never met anyone she'd worked with before. Marcy kept that part of her life separate from her personal life."

"Cassie, I'm just curious, if you would oblige me."

"Sure, knock yourself out."

"Have you always been into women?"

Cassie looked off into the distance, marinating on Raven's question. She wasn't quite sure how to respond, so she responded with a simple, "No," in hopes that Raven wouldn't push the issue. But, she wasn't feeling that lucky at the moment.

"So you dated men before?"

"Yes," she answered reluctantly. "I didn't come here to talk about me, though. I wanted to talk about Marcy."

"Well, you were part of Marcy's life, so why *not* talk about you?"

"Are you curious?"

"Maybe"

"Yeah, right!"

"No, really, I'm curious."

"So, you're telling me you want to experience a woman?"

"Well, actually, I've been down that road before," Raven smirked.

"So then your curiosity was satisfied."

"Okay, check this. Forget all of that lesbo shit, 'cause really I'm not interested in pussy. However, what I *am* interested in is getting back at Jay Dawson."

Cassie sat her cup on the table. "Jay Dawson?"

"Yes, you know him. He's the man you fucked away from Marcy, your so-called friend," Raven snapped. "So, you can cut that 'wanting to know about Marcy' shit out."

Cassie squared her shoulders and looked Raven directly in the eyes. "Yes, Jay had an affair with me while he was dating Marcy, and then…"

"Cut the explanation. I know all of the grimy details. You fucked her man, felt awful, and then made friends with her. But, instead of being her friend, you ended up fucking her, too. You are truly a sick bitch!"

"You don't know what you're talking about. I loved Marcy," she said sternly. "And I don't…no, I won't sit here and allow you to insult me."

Raven felt awful for a minute, but that feeling dissipated quickly. "Listen, I'll stop beating around the bush. I believe in being upfront. This way, there will be no confusion, and if you choose you want to roll with it, then cool."

"I beg your pardon?"

"Jay Dawson jilted me and he has to pay."

"Pay?"

"Yes, a very high price."

Cassie broke out in hysterical laughter. "Yes, you are sick."

"Do you find me attractive, Cassie?"

Cassie's laughter turned to a look of confusion. "Do you think all lesbians have a thing for every woman they meet?"

Raven smirked and casually leaned back in her seat. "I've been with Marcy."

Cassie's look of confusion turned to anger. There were touches of humor around Raven's mouth and near her eyes that intrigued Cassie. She was actually contemplating the question. Did she find Raven attractive? Of course, she did. But would she act on that attraction? Probably not.

"Something is wrong with you," she snapped, grabbing her belongings and standing to her feet. "This little…meeting is over."

Raven leaned forward and grabbed Cassie by the wrist. "I didn't mean to offend you."

"You know what I get sick and tired of? I get sick and tired of people assuming that because I prefer to spend my time with women, I'm out to lick every pussy that walks down the street. Well guess what, Raven? Just as a brother is picky about the pussy he dives into, so am I."

Cassie snatched her wrist from Raven's clutch. "Besides, I wouldn't want to turn you out. Now, if you'll excuse me." Cassie turned on her heels, held her head high, and headed out the door and toward her vehicle. However, Raven was quickly on her heels.

Cassie could hear Raven's footsteps quickly approaching. Her heart began to race rapidly, not from fear, but from the anticipation of giving in to her. Deep down inside, she wanted to be with her, but it was silly, she thought.

Cassie fumbled in her purse for her keys, which tumbled from her hands to the ground. Raven quickly snatched them up and dangled them before her.

Their eyes boldly met. Raven took a step closer. She could smell Cassie's scent of sandalwood, a fragrance that was arousing her. "Okay, I get it. You're an old-fashioned sister." Raven licked and puckered her lips and cooed, "Would you prefer dinner first?"

"Yes, as a matter of fact, I would prefer dinner, conversation, a few dates, an AIDS test, and anything else you can think of before you try and dance with me."

"Oooh, feisty, just how I like it."

Cassie reached for her keys and snatched them from Raven's grasp. "Look, you're bothering me."

Raven took a step backward. She wasn't sure about what she was doing, but she was confident about one thing. She liked Cassie and she wanted to be with her. She didn't know where all of this was coming from — these feelings and thoughts of wanting to share herself with a woman. For years, she'd been strictly about the dick and there was going to be no changing it, but she didn't mind adding a little spice to her life.

"Fine, I'll leave you alone."

When Raven turned to walk away, Cassie opened her mouth, as if she was going to speak. Then suddenly, her mouth closed and she got into her car. She was interested, but she wasn't sure how to take Raven. She was coming on a little too strong for her taste. She'd never been approached in such a manner and was feeling uncomfortable. *What the hell,* she thought. "Raven!" she yelled out. "Have you ever heard of foreplay?"

"Yes, I love their music," Raven smiled. Her apprehension abated somewhat under the warm glow of her smile. The beginning of a smile tipped the corners of Cassie's mouth. "You have a beautiful smile."

"Thank you. Can we start over?" Cassie asked, biting on her bottom lip.

Raven's lips curved into a smirk. She leaned down and into the car, softly pressing her lips against Cassie's cheek. "I would like that."

"Get in," Cassie ordered, and Raven rushed around to the passenger side of her car. "Let's go to my place. We can talk there."

"Sounds good to me."

Cassie inserted the key into her front door. "Would you like some coffee?"

"Not unless we're planning on being up all night," she chuckled.

"Well, I don't have any alcohol. I don't drink the hard stuff. But there may be a bottle of wine in the fridge."

"I'm fine," Raven said, following Cassie into the living room and watching her behind sway from side to side. She smiled and shook her head with delight. She was going to enjoy caressing that ass. Raven didn't know what was going on with her, and she didn't care. For that moment, she was feeling in control and wanted to experience the passion she felt with Marcy.

"Get comfortable," Cassie offered, "while I get out of these shoes. My feet are killing me."

Raven stood in the middle of the floor and watched her as she disappeared into the bedroom. She slipped off her leather jacket and started to lay it across the sofa, but quickly changed her mind and draped it across her arm instead.

The sofa was white as snow, as well as the other furniture. Cassie's apartment looked more like a showplace than a place to relax. The only splash of color was a huge, beautiful art piece by Charles Bibbs hanging over the sofa. She was really digging Cassie's taste, but it didn't feel too homey to her.

"I'll be out in a minute," Cassie yelled from the back. "Help yourself to whatever is in the fridge."

Raven draped her jacket over the back of the dining room chair, which was also white , but by this time, she didn't care. *Why have furniture you can't sit on,* she thought, then she slithered into the kitchen and peeked into the refrigerator. She reached in and pulled out a bottle of wine she'd never heard of before, *JazzBerry* by Boordy Vineyards. She thought the bottle was interesting because of its unique label. It was the first time she'd seen a wine bottle with people partying on the label. She shrugged her shoulders, searched the kitchen cabinets for two wine glasses, and headed for the dining room, sitting the glasses on the glass-topped dining room table. She peered down at the two lion statues holding the glass top in place. Something she would've never thought to do, but interesting nonetheless. She popped the cork and partially filled the glasses.

Raven wondered what was taking Cassie so long. "You have a nice place," she shouted. She needed to hurry this along because her desire to be intimate with Cassie was beginning to dissipate. "Are you going to be much longer?"

After a fifteen-minute wait, Cassie finally graced Raven with her presence. "That wasn't too long, was it?"

"I thought I was going to have to call in the National Guard," Raven chuckled.

"Yes, well, I needed to unwind for a minute. It's been a long day." Cassie nervously nodded toward the glasses sitting on the table. "I see you found the wine."

"Yes, I hope you don't mind. I thought we both could use a glass…to unwind."

Cassie reached for the glass of wine and pressed the rim against her lips, flinging her head back as the red sweet liquid flowed down her throat.

Raven looked at her in astonishment. Cassie extended her glass toward Raven. As she began to pour, Cassie said, "To the rim, please."

Raven's eyes left the glass and darted toward Cassie. *Not a damn lush,* she thought. She wasn't interested in a woman who had to drink to get herself in the mood.

After two more full-to-the-rim glasses of wine, Cassie inhaled and exhaled, with a long sigh following. "Well, are you ready?"

"Ready for what?"

"Ready to love me."

Raven glared into her eyes. They were quite glossy, reminiscent of a drunkard. Now, her desire to explore Cassie was null and she was no longer interested. Still, she'd come that far, so she was going to see it through. Plus, her bud needed some attention.

"Cassie, how about a little music?"

"Sure, what's your pleasure?"

"Something soft."

Cassie walked over to the stereo system, opened the CD drawer, and inserted a CD. When Cassie bent over, Raven cringed as she salivated at the beauty of Cassie's posterior. Raven's thighs began to feel heavy and her sex was damp.

Alicia Keys belted out, "I can give you diamonds," as Cassie swung her hips from side to side in a titillating rhythm. "I really love this song," Cassie said, really getting into the music, her body heaving and her hardened nipples protruding through her silk blouse. "Hell, I love all of her songs."

"The sister is very talented, and attractive to boot."

Cassie's eyes roamed the room and then she took a seat on the sofa. "Let's have a seat." She patted the empty space beside her. "I don't bite, Raven."

Raven chuckled and sat beside Cassie. She was no longer feeling in control. Her palms were sweaty and her stomach had butterflies. She was nervous as hell.

Cassie cupped her by the face and pulled her in close. "Relax," she said, brushing their lips together. The hairs on the back of Raven's neck stood to attention. "Relax, baby," she whispered in her ear. The tense lines on Raven's face disappeared and her body relaxed in Cassie's embrace.

Cassie grabbed her by the waist and pulled her closer. Raven slightly moaned. Cassie gently kissed her, sliding her hand under Raven's blouse and cupping her breast. Raven's body stiffened from her touch as the throbbing between her thighs intensified. She flinched at every caress and pinch made on her half-dollar nipples. She couldn't control the spasmodic trembling within her. With a swift motion, her blouse was eased over her head and tossed to the floor. Cassie removed Raven's bra and knelt down before her, parting Raven's legs and pushing her skirt above her waist. She continued to stroke Raven's nipples with her tongue and then trailed down to her chocolate cove and lightly blew.

A delightful shiver of Raven wanting Cassie ran through her. Cassie slithered her tongue through Raven's opening and feasted on her essence. Raven felt the blood surge from the top of her head to the tips of her toes. Her body heaved and her breast jutted upward as Cassie's finger entered through Raven's juices, finding her sensitive spot. She raised her arms above her head and stretched.

"Oooh," Raven cooed, causing Cassie's nipples to stiffen. "That feels so good, Cass." She moved her hips in a slow, circular motion. "Hmmm," she moaned.

For six months, Cassie had been experiencing menopause and her desire for sex had gone down the drain after Marcy's death, or so she had thought. But Raven had brought her back to life.

Cassie looked up at her. "Come down here," she said, pulling Raven down to her side. She exposed her breast. "Kiss it for me." Raven leaned in and puckered her pink lips. She inhaled and smiled to herself. Cassie's fragrance of sandalwood was more intense. As she gently kissed Cassie's firm nipple, she cupped her breast in her hand. Cassie's head fell backward, her heart jolted, and her pulse pounded as Raven took her breast in her mouth. "Damn, woman," Cassie moaned.

Cassie lay back on the floor and pulled Raven on top of her. Their lips caressed and tongues played. "I want to taste you," Raven panted. She wormed down before Cassie's abdomen, unzipped her pants, and pulled them down around her ankles. Cassie freed her feet from the hostage of her pants and spread her legs apart as wide as she could.

Raven stared at her sex and smiled. "You have a pretty puss."

Cassie smiled and raised her legs in the air. "How about my ass?"

"I noticed that a long time ago."

"Hmm," Cassie moaned as she fingered herself.

Raven leaned in and inhaled. She was no fool. She wanted to make sure Cassie kept herself clean. She wasn't eating anybody's fish.

Cassie tilted her hips upward and beckoned Raven. Raven closed her eyes and stuck out her tongue. Cassie pushed her hips into Raven's face and giggled. "Don't be afraid. I'll do you next."

Raven defended herself. "I'm not afraid." She was eager to be on the receiving end and grabbed Cassie by the hips, holding her down as she sucked on her bud profusely, bringing her to a quick climax.

Raven quickly flipped over and spread her legs. "It's your turn."

"Well damn," Cassie laughed. "Alright, but give me one second."

"Why?"

"I'll be right back." Cassie disappeared into the bedroom and returned with a chocolate-colored strap-on dildo. Raven's eyes bulged and her excitement grew. Cassie stood over Raven, strapped the apparatus around her waist, and then dropped to her knees, assuming the doggy position. She leaned into Raven and consumed her. Raven's hips twitched and wiggled, trying to escape from

Cassie's grip. Raven felt like she was ready to explode. Cassie secured Raven's hips and locked down on them as tight as she could.

Raven hated the feeling of being tied down. She desperately tried to wiggle free, but Cassie's strength was beyond hers. "Okay, okay…don't hold me down!" Raven hollered. "I can't stand that! Don't do it!"

Cassie released her hold and rose up on her knees. "Hey, I'm sorry. I didn't mean to make you feel uncomfortable. I only wanted you to feel good."

"It's not you. I have this thing about being held down. It feels kind of claustrophobic. You know what I mean?"

Cassie nodded and smiled. "Again, I'm sorry."

"No need to apologize." She nodded toward her sex. "Can we finish?"

Cassie chuckled, then leaned down and kissed Raven on the lips, forming a trail down to her belly button. The caress of Cassie's lips on her mouth and along her body set her aflame. Gently, Cassie eased the rubber apparatus into her opening. Raven drew her abdomen into Cassie. Raven's hands slowly moved downward, skimming both sides of her body to her thighs, down to the apparatus where she slipped her finger underneath to the opening of her lips, searching for her pleasure points. She continuously flicked her swollen bud with her finger until they both climaxed.

Cassie lay beside her as she leaned over and, with her tongue, stroked her hardened nipple down to her opening. Without thought, Raven spread her legs and wrapped them around Cassie's neck as she nestled her head in her cave and sipped her delectable juices.

Chapter 47

The teakettle whistled as Morgan reached in the cupboard for a cup. "You still didn't tell me how you fell in bed with my sister."

"I told you before. She blackmailed me with Reneè Jarvis. She told me she would tell you all about Renceè if I didn't give her what she wanted."

Morgan poured the hot tea into the cup and placed it before Arthur. "Lemon and honey?"

"Yes, thank you."

After retrieving a whole lemon and a jar of honey from the refrigerator, Morgan grabbed a knife from the utensil drawer and pulled up a seat across from Arthur at the kitchen table. She looked at the knife and then at him. She contemplated lunging across the table and slashing his throat, but she thought twice. Fortunately for him, she loved him. She also knew that no matter how tough he tried to carry himself, Arthur was truly a weak man.

She slowly inserted the knife into the lemon and sliced with precision. "How did she kill them and get away with it?"

"I've been trying to figure that one out, too. According to the news reports…"

She dropped a lemon slice in Arthur's cup. "News reports? It made the news?"

"Yes, Morgan. If you watched the news, you would've heard about it."

She grabbed the jar of honey and cut her eyes at him. "You're in no position to be a smart ass, Mr. Adulterer," she snapped, twisting the top off the jar and pouring honey into each cup.

Arthur stood and paced the floor. "So what are we going to do?"

"I don't know." Morgan sipped her tea and glanced at Franklin sitting in the infant seat propped up on the table. "He's so beautiful. Isn't he?"

Arthur proudly looked at his son and smiled. "Yes, he is." He dropped his hands to his sides and stared at Morgan. "I don't want to lose my family. I don't want to lose you. I love you so much, it hurts."

A smirk crossed her lips and she gently nodded her head. "Where was all of that pain of love when you were sleeping with my sister?"

"Damn it, Morgan, you know how your sister can be," he snapped. "I was vulnerable, didn't know what to do. That woman wouldn't let me alone."

She slammed her hand on the table in anger. "Then why didn't you come to me? You come to me to bitch and complain about everything else!"

"Because I didn't want to hurt you," he yelled.

"Why are *you* yelling? I didn't betray you, Arthur. You betrayed me, or did you forget so quickly!"

Arthur's shoulders slouched, yet he still stood firmly in his place. "I'm coming to you now, honey."

"Yeah, a day late and…"

"You know, this is why I didn't come to you in the first place. You wouldn't know how to handle it. I went to Raven because I knew she had it in her to handle that type of situation."

Morgan's mouth fell open as she stood to her feet. "Well, I'll be damned." She leaned over and kissed Franklin's forehead. "How dare you turn this mess around on me?"

"That's not what I'm doing. Look, I take full responsibility for my actions. I fucked up and I know this, and I'm sure there isn't anything I can do, as far as you're concerned, that will rectify things..."

"Yes, there's something you can do. My little sister must be taught a valuable lesson."

"What's the lesson?"

"She has this idiotic saying, 'do unto others before they do unto her.' Perhaps, the saying should be, 'do unto yourself as you've done to others.'"

Arthur pulled up a chair, looking confused, "What are you talking about, Morgan?"

"What did she do to Ramone?"

"I wasn't in the room, so I don't know exactly."

"You didn't see it at all?"

"Well, as she was coming out of the room, I did get a glance over her shoulder. Ramone was face down, tied to the bedposts, and Reneè was face-up. They both had pillows over their heads."

Morgan shook her head in disbelief. "Damn, that bitch is psychotic. I knew Raven was capable of many things, but murder...I just can't seem to fathom it."

"What about your parents?"

"I don't think she intended for them to die."

Arthur grunted and rested his chin in the span of his hand, peering at her. "I can tell your mind is at work."

Morgan poked out her lips, and then twisted them upward. "Raven needs a good old fashioned ass whipping."

Arthur laughed. "Yeah, she needs to be taken out to the woodshed."

"Something like that," she pondered. "Watch Franklin. I need to pay my *sister* a visit." Morgan kissed Franklin's cheek and dashed for the front door.

"What are you going to do?" Arthur yelled after her.

"I'm going to go and whip her ass," she yelled as the door slammed behind her.

Chapter 48

Jo was in heaven. Last night with Chas was off the chain. He surprised her with the best sex she'd ever experienced. It was nice, too. It wasn't the rough kind of sex, where her knees would be pushed back to her ears or the man pounding against her behind like a jackhammer, and then in the morning, she'd be soaking in a bath of Epsom salt because her legs and ass would be sore as hell. No, it was soft and gentle. She felt as silky as his silk sheets, and she loved waking up to him in the morning. It was definitely something she could get used to.

"That brother got your nose so wide open, I can see your brain," Dora chuckled as she and Jo shopped in Pentagon City.

"I don't know what you're talking about," Jo blushed, blurting out a schoolgirl giggle. She stopped abruptly in front of the window of Macy's. "How do you think Chas would look in that sweater?"

Dora turned her mouth up and kicked out her foot. "I hardly think you need to start buying his clothes."

"I'm not *buying* his clothes, Missy. His birthday is coming up."

Jo had just told the biggest lie, and Dora knew it. She knew her best friend all too well and that she couldn't lie worth a damn. "Look at me, Jo."

Jo didn't budge. "What?"

"When is that man's birthday?"

"Huh?"

"That's what I figured. Seems like to me you can't stay out of the bed long enough to ask him."

"Don't hate on me, Grouchy."

"Ain't nobody hating on you, and I've told you about that 'Grouchy' stuff."

Jo made a beeline for Anne Taylor Loft. After entering the store, she picked up a peach cashmere sweater and held it against her. "What do you think?"

"Makes you look washed out."

Jo tossed the sweater to the side and picked up the same cashmere, but in red. "How about this one?"

"Yeah, red's more your color."

Jo smiled and hung the sweater over her arm. "Now I need to find a pair of pants."

"Not in here you won't," Dora chuckled. "You're far from having a petite behind."

"You've got a point there."

"So, Jo, tell me more about Chas."

"Dora, he's wonderful. I think I'm falling for him."

"You mean in love?"

Jo nodded her head and moved toward the register. "Girl, that man leaves me speechless."

"I'm happy for you, Jo. But, don't you think you're moving a little too fast?"

"Probably, but hell, I ain't getting any younger and my biological clock is ticking away."

"Does he talk about future planning? Does he want kids?"

"We haven't talked about it."

"Don't you think you should?"

"Girl, look, I'm not making any plans. I'm just living in the moment."

"Well, that's good. Hey, let's go to Victoria's Secret."

"Good idea. I need to pick up new panties."

"Nasty hoe," Dora blurted out.

Jo fell out with laughter. "I keep telling you to stop hating on me."

Dora rolled her eyes.

They made a beeline to Victoria's Secret. Afterwards, they lunched at the Food Court and decided to take in a movie.

Chapter 49

A deep male voice, slow like thick molasses, spoke into her ear. "How did it go?"

"Just as we planned," Cassie smiled.

"I knew it. That trick can't pass up getting fucked, whether by male or female."

"It was easier than I had expected."

"So, did you enjoy her?"

"Can't say that I enjoyed *her*, but I did enjoy the act," she chuckled. "Still, the bitch has to pay. So, I'll do whatever I have to do. You feel me?"

"Yeah, I feel you."

"So, what's next?"

Jay sighed heavily into the receiver. "It's time to bring it home."

"Then we'll focus on us, right?"

"Right, baby girl."

"So, what's the plan?"

"You think you can get her back to your place?"

"Oh yeah…old' girl is more than willing. Hell, I didn't think she was going to leave," Cassie laughed. "Ms. Raven has been officially turned out."

"Good, that's real good. It's going to go down Friday night, your place."

"Okay, what do you need me to do?"

"Clean your place and go with the flow. We're having a party," he chuckled. "I'll take care of everything."

"I'll call her, invite her over…what time?"

"Nine o'clock is good. I'll have my people there by seven. Cool?"

"Cool."

Chapter 50

Raven sat on the toilet for what seemed like an eternity. Her legs were numb and her behind was sore. She leaned on her thighs and stared blankly at the floor. She pushed down as hard as she could, trying to rid herself of her experience with Cassie. She had enjoyed it and that bothered her. She desperately wanted to talk to Morgan, but that wasn't going to happen since Morgan had her ass up on her shoulders. She didn't know why Morgan was treating her so badly. She hadn't done anything to he, besides sleep with her husband, and she knew Morgan didn't know about her escapades with Arthur.

Before Raven could rationalize why Morgan was acting so funny, her phone rang. She tore a few sheets of toilet paper from the roll, neatly folded the sheets, and gently wiped her tender vagina. Cassie had just about sucked her raw. When she rose to her feet, her head felt woozy. The phone continued to ring. She grabbed hold of the sink, trying to keep from spinning with the room. Finally able to stand erect, she darted from the bathroom to the kitchen and snatched the phone from the receiver.

"Yes, hello," she panted.

"You're still out of breath? I'm glad to see I have that affect on you," Cassie chuckled.

"What's up?" Raven wasn't amused at Cassie's cockiness.

"I was calling to see if you have any plans for Friday night around nine o'clock."

'Nothing I can't cancel."

"Great. I'm having a little gathering at my place and I would love to show you off to my friends."

"Show me off?"

"Yes, I want you to meet my friends."

"I'm not your girlfriend…or boyfriend…or whatever."

"No one said that you were."

"Good, as long as we are on the same page. We spent one evening together and that was it."

Cassie became annoyed at Raven's nonchalant attitude. "So, you're saying the evening we spent meant nothing to you? I gave you my all, Raven. I loved you the same way I would love my woman."

"Why are you getting so pissy? I thought we were on the same page?"

"I don't mind being on your page, Raven, so long as you aren't disrespectful and inconsiderate of my feelings."

"What feelings? Now you're getting your feelings involved? Now I see why niggers don't fuck with bitches."

Cassie gasped. She was ready to chew Raven a new asshole, but she had to remain focused on the task at hand, which was getting Raven to her place Friday night. "Listen, I don't want to argue." Cassie bit her bottom lip. "Besides, I want to see you again. So, see you Friday?"

"Yeah, sure, I'll see you Friday. Anything I can bring?"

"Nope, just you."

A knock at the door startled her. "Someone's at my door. I'll call you later." When Raven approached the door, she realized she didn't have on any pants. "Just a second." She ran to her bedroom and slipped into a terry cloth robe. "I'm coming!" She stood on the tips of her toes and peeped through the peephole. A bouquet of white lilies blocked her view. "Chas," she exclaimed as she opened the door.

"Not quite," the voice behind the bouquet said.

The voice was right. Whoever was behind the bouquet was too short for Chas.

"May I help you?"

"Maybe," the voice said as the bouquet was extended toward her. "How are you, Raven?"

"Oh my God!"

"It's been a long time."

"What are you doing here?"

"Can't I visit an old friend?" Raven stood speechless. She never thought she would ever see him again. "Aren't you going to ask me in?"

Her feet wouldn't move from where she stood. She couldn't believe her eyes. He was still short, but no longer fat. Where did all of those muscles come from? She examined him from head to toe. Was that an Armani suit?

"At least take the flowers," he chuckled.

"Michael Anthony?"

"In the flesh and one hundred fifty pounds lighter." Raven managed to move and stepped back for him to enter. "I see you're still looking beautiful."

"Th-thanks," she stuttered. "Uh, have a seat. Can I get you anything?"

"No, thank you. I'm fine."

Raven sat the flowers on the coffee table. "They are beautiful. Thank you."

"You're welcome. You seem like the lily type of woman."

Raven smiled to hide her being uncomfortable. "You look really good, Michael." This was not the same Michael Anthony who previously darkened her doorstep with stubby fingers and two hundred and fifty pounds. No longer was he short, fat, and disgusting. Instead, he was still short, but muscular, toned, and good looking. "You look great, Michael. What brings you all the way from Cleveland?"

Michael crossed his legs and rested his hand on his knee. He looked down and briefly stared at the floor. "I came here for you."

"Uh, you did?"

With his head still down, his eyes rolled up toward his brow. "I wanted you to see what you had missed out on."

"Michael, I'm glad you stopped by and I'm sorry for all of the drama that went on between us, but I think you should leave."

"Is this how you treat someone who brought you such beautiful flowers?" He rose to his feet.

Raven remained calm and managed to speak through stiff lips. "I don't want any trouble."

He walked toward her, leaned down, and stared at her blankly, his eyes looking almost crossed. "I don't want any trouble, either. I wanted to personally tell you how fucked up you really are, and if you don't watch, you're going to get what's due to you."

Raven jumped to her feet, grabbed him by the elbow, and roughly escorted him to the door. She flung the door open and proclaimed, "You could look like Morris Chestnut and I still wouldn't want your short, nasty ass," and shoved him into the hallway, slamming the door in his face. "He's still a short motherfucker!"

Chapter 51

The next hour crawled by at a snail's pace. Morgan's eyes were closed tight and her hands gripped the steering wheel with all of her strength as she sat at the traffic light. If that steering wheel were Raven's neck, she would've snapped it in two. She leaned her head against the headrest and relaxed her tensed muscles. The screaming horn to the rear of her startled her.

"Alright, damn it! Hold your horses!" She held her tears in check as she sped down the street toward Raven's complex. She whizzed past the South East Waterfront, made a sharp turn into the complex and stopped abruptly. She slapped the gear in park and stared aimlessly at the sliding glass door to Raven's condominium. Raven walked about her living, without a care in the world, as Morgan breathed anger. Her eyes darted around the car for anything she could get her hands on that would inflict just as much pain as was inflicted on her. Her eyes rested on her cell phone charging in the cigarette lighter. She unplugged the cell from the charger and snatched the cord from the cigarette lighter. Then, she tossed her purse on the floor and got out the car. Her eyes glossed over as she marched up the stairs and stopped before Raven's front door. She wiped her eyes with the back of her hands and proceeded to knock.

Raven peeked through the peephole and released a slight giggle. She hadn't seen her sister in quite some time. She opened the door and reached for Morgan, taking her into a warm, sisterly embrace. Morgan didn't return the warmth.

"Hey, big sis. I haven't seen you in so long, I almost forgot what you look like. Come on in." Morgan looked past her and gripped the cord tightly in her clutch. "So, what brings you here? Where's Franklin? I still haven't spent time with my nephew and godson."

Morgan wandered motionlessly toward the recliner, looking around before taking a seat. As usual, Raven's place was a sty. "Franklin is home with his father, *my* husband."

Raven detected the sarcasm in her voice. "Oh," she uttered and sat down on the sofa directly across from Morgan.

Morgan looked around again and commented, "No drawers in the corner. That's unusual." Raven raised her brow in confusion. "Usually, when I come here, I have to step over nasty drawers and condom wrappers."

"What's your problem?" Raven asked with a twist of her neck. "And you've never seen condom wrappers on my floor," she shot back.

Morgan leaned over and rested her elbows on her thighs. She pursed her lips together and spoke through clinched teeth. "You stay away from *my* husband. Do you hear me?"

Raven leaned back and crossed her legs. "What in the hell are you talking about, Morgan?"

Morgan's body heated up and her veins were about to pop. "Don't insult my intelligence!" Morgan jumped to her feet. "I saw you…I saw you fuck my husband!"

Raven tilted her chin up and smiled at Morgan. "Are you experiencing postpartum something or another, because you are straight trippin'?"

"Oh, cut the bullshit, Raven. You know I know you better than anyone. You continue to try, but you can't pull the wool over my eyes."

"Arthur is lying. Don't you see that he's lying?" Raven fluidly rose to her feet, straightening her shoulders. She was always in control and was determined to control this situation, as well. Morgan didn't know what she was talking about, as far as she was concerned. Arthur came on to her and she was going to convince Morgan of that, if it was the last thing she'd do. "He came on to me. I told him I couldn't do that to you, but he insisted."

Morgan turned her back to her. "Raven, give it up. This time, things won't conform to you. Arthur told me everything." She leaned her head back and sighed. "I know about Reneè, Ramone, and you."

"But Morgan," Raven stuttered. She had lost control. "I did it for you."

Morgan swung herself around. "You did it for me?"

"Yes, I did it for you. If I hadn't intervened, he would've had an affair on you."

Morgan took an abrupt step toward her. "You are sick! You're not happy until you've fucked up someone's life."

"I love you, sis. I mean, I kept him from being with her. Don't you see that?" Morgan stretched her eyes wide and her mouth dropped to the floor. "See, him being with me worked out. I am your sister, so if he has sex with me, it's not adultery. But, had he done it with Reneè, it would've been and I knew that would've really hurt you." Morgan couldn't believe what she was hearing. "You know how we do, Mo," she smiled. "We're keeping it in the family. You know, what's yours is mine and vice versa. Don't act like you've never wanted to experience Ramone or even Chas."

Morgan closed her eyes and swung at Raven as hard as she could, knocking her upside the head. Raven fell back against the sofa. "You bitch! You stay away from me and my family," she yelled loudly as she whipped Raven's ass with the cord. Raven was defenseless against Morgan's powerful blows. Raven balled up into a fetal position, crying for Morgan to stop. The last blow struck Raven across her face, leaving a deep gash. Morgan stepped back and looked at her. "You ain't shit, Raven. Don't you ever, I mean as long as you live, speak to me again. I have no sister. You stay the fuck away from my husband, or the next time, I'll put a fucking bullet in your head. Or, better yet, I'll have your ass locked up for life for killing Reneè and Ramone. Do you hear me?"

Raven nodded and cried profusely. "I'm so sorry, Morgan."

Morgan stood over Raven, panting. Hot tears rolled down her cheeks. Her mouth trembled as she started to speak. "No, you're not sorry for what you've done. It's not in you to be sorry for anything. You're selfish. You don't care about anyone but yourself. You better be careful, girl. What comes around goes around, and you will get yours...one day." Morgan dropped the cord on the coffee table and walked toward the door. She heaved as she cried, taking one last look at the sister she had, at one time, loved more than her own life. "Stay away from me," she said softly as the door closed behind her.

Chapter 52

Raven finished off the last drop of Hennessy. She wasn't in the mood for Cassie's party, but she needed to do something to clear her mind of Morgan. It had been three days since their altercation. She tried calling Arthur, but his cell phone number had been changed, as well as the house number. She'd contemplated showing up at their house, but thought twice about it. As tough as she thought she was, she knew better than to go up against Morgan. Surprisingly, though, she felt no remorse for her extracurricular activities with Arthur. She did nothing wrong, and, therefore, there was no reason for her to feel as if she did. Somewhere in Raven's sick, demented mind, she honestly felt she wasn't the other woman. She felt, deep inside, she was doing Morgan a favor. After all, since they were sisters, Arthur having sex with her was different than him having sex with Renee. They did come from the same seed, right? They have the same blood running through their veins, right? They are sisters and sisters share. Twins did it all the time, as far as she was concerned, so why couldn't they?

In a drunken haze, she turned on the shower. While standing before the mirror, she ran her finger down the gash that Morgan slashed in her face with the end of the cord. She couldn't retaliate against Morgan. She loved her too much.

She eased out of her clothes and stepped her drunken behind into the shower. She reached for the shower gel, squeezed a large amount onto the loofah sponge, and lathered around her neck, over her breasts, circling her abdomen, between her thighs, down her legs, and to the bottoms of her feet. She slowly backed into the stream of water, leaned her head back, and closed her eyes. Dizziness overcame her. She lost her balance and grabbed hold to the shower curtain. With the shower curtain rings not being strong enough to hold her, each ring popped off the curtain rod and she lost her footing, falling out of the tub. She tumbled downward, her head connecting with the porcelain toilet and then with the tile floor. Blood splattered from her mouth to the floor and walls. Her body slithered from the tub and onto the floor, where she lay in a pool of karma. She inhaled deeply and released her last breath.

Visit Jessica Tilles
at
www.jessicatilles.com.

Send comments to:
JessicaTilles@aol.com.

Novels by Jessica Tilles

_____ *Anything Goes*, ISBN: 0-9722990-0-9
$15.00

_____ *In My Sisters' Corner*, ISBN: 0-9722990-1-7
$15.00

_____ *Apple Tree*, ISBN: 0-9722990-2-5
$15.00

_____ *Sweet Revenge*, ISBN: 0-9722990-3-3
$15.00

Maryland residents, add 5% sales tax to your order.

Send to:
Xpress Yourself Publishing
P.O. Box 1615
Upper Marlboro, MD 20773

Please send me the books I have checked above. I am
enclosing $_____ (plus 5% sales tax for Maryland
residents). Send check or money order — no cash or
C.O.D.s please. Allow up to two weeks for delivery.

Name _____

Address _____

City _____ State/Zip _____

Autograph to _____